CAST OF CHARACTERS

FAMILY SECRETS

In Emerald Cove, blood is thicker than water.

Laura Evans—She finally has the chance to validate her career to her family, but will it put her life—and her heart—in jeopardy?

Austin Brady—Drawn to adventure, the thrill-seeking journalist is about to discover a fluff piece on a sexy marine biologist could be the most intriguing assignment of his career.

Gretchen Wagner—Genetically engineered to possess superhuman code-cracking abilities, can she figure out who's hacking into the Evans Yachts computer system?

Holt Evans—He's been gearing up for the annual regatta, but does this playboy have what it takes to win the race...and save the family's reputation?

About the Author

JUDITH LYONS

lives deep in the Wisconsin woods where the summers are short and the winters long and cold. Reading and writing romances is the best way she knows to stay sane during those long, frigid months. She lives there with her husband, teenage daughter and their small menagerie of dogs, cat, birds and fish. As avid divers, their favorite vacation locations are those that are warm…and deep.

The FAMILY SECRETS continuity was Judith's first continuity, and she was thrilled to be asked on board such an exciting, innovative project. Not only did the series offer cutting-edge plots, but her heroine was a marine biologist! Through this character Judith was able to share a world she loves—the wonderful reefs and their fascinating, colorful inhabitants—with her readers.

CLOSE QUARTERS

JUDITH LYONS

Published by Silhouette Books

America's Publisher of Contemporary Romance

Special thanks and acknowledgment are given to Judith Lyons for her contribution to the FAMILY SECRETS series.

SILHOUETTE BOOKS

ISBN 0-373-61382-2

CLOSE QUARTERS

Copyright © 2003 by Harlequin Books S.A.

This edition published by arrangement with Harlequin Books S.A.

® and TM are trademarks of Harlequin Books S.A., used under license. Trademarks indicated with ® are registered in the United States Patent and Trademark Office, the Canadian Trade Marks Office and in other countries.

Visit us at www.silhouettefamilysecrets.com

Printed in U.S.A.

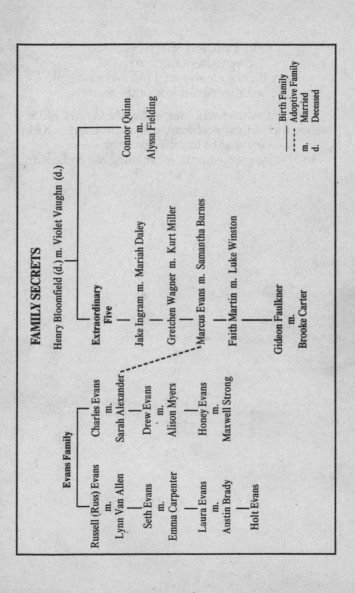

FAMILY SECRETS

Henry Bloomfield (d.) m. Violet Vaughn (d.)

Extraordinary Five

Connor Quinn
m.
Alyssa Fielding

Jake Ingram m. Mariah Daley

Gretchen Wagner m. Kurt Miller

Marcus Evans m. Samantha Barnes

Faith Martin m. Luke Winston

Gideon Faulkner
m.
Brooke Carter

Evans Family

Russell (Russ) Evans
m.
Lynn Van Allen

Charles Evans
m.
Sarah Alexander

Seth Evans
m.
Emma Carpenter

Drew Evans
m.
Alison Myers

Laura Evans
m.
Austin Brady

Honey Evans
m.
Maxwell Strong

Holt Evans

——— Birth Family
– – – Adoptive Family
m. Married
d. Deceased

To Barb and Terry Spennetta,
divemasters extraordinaire.
Many thanks for showing me and my family
the other two-thirds of the world!

To all the editors who made the FAMILY SECRETS
series such an extraordinary project. You ladies rock.
Many thanks for all your hard work.
And many, *many* thanks for inviting me on board.

One

Austin Brady sat in his rental car, the air-conditioning going full blast as he stared at the tiny, dilapidated stucco house sitting back from the pock-marked black rocks that defined the Gulf coast's edge.

Huh.

Maybe he had the wrong address. He glanced at the numbers and street name he'd scrawled on a scrap of paper this morning in the hotel and compared it to the address stenciled on the dented mailbox next to his car. Right address.

He looked back to the ramshackle home. Maybe the place was just a workstation. He sure couldn't imagine the daughter of one of Florida's richest families *living* here. As a freelance photojournalist he'd profiled plenty of the rich—both the famous and the not so famous. While many of them liked their adventures as wild and rugged as nature and man's imagination could provide and a few of them even worked in harsh conditions, at the end of the day they all returned to the lap of luxury. He couldn't imagine Laura Evans, the subject of his next article, being any different. At least he hadn't counted on her being any different when he'd agreed to this job.

He pulled into the small, circular driveway nestled beside the house, the sound of crushed shells crunching beneath his tires. He parked next to the blue Taurus station wagon sitting beside the house and got out of his car. The heat and humidity of Florida in August draped over him like a hot, wet blanket. He peeked into the back of the station wagon. A couple of air tanks and loose diving gear lay haphazardly in the back. He definitely had the right place.

He climbed the three cement stairs leading to the small porch, taking in the stained walls and overgrown weedy lawn. The place didn't look any more inviting up close than it had from his car. Caleb, Caleb, Caleb, what have you gotten me into, old buddy? If you've stuck me in some tiny shack in the middle of nowhere with some homely academic, I'm going to wring your neck.

And Laura Evans would be homely. In his experience, beautiful, rich women didn't devote their lives to research. They donned obscenely expensive clothes, coiffed their hair and sashayed into the world to socialize. Only homely rich women looked outside the social whirl for something to occupy their time.

He knocked on the door.

When no one answered, he glanced at his watch. Okay, he was an hour early. If this *was* a workstation, maybe she just hadn't arrived yet. But her car was here. He leaned closer to the door, shadowing the glass so he could peer in. The place was filled with furniture. And it had a definite homey air. Damn.

He'd taken this assignment because he thought he'd be staying in a big, fancy house where he'd spend his days sitting beside a pool in the shade of a palm tree sipping cool drinks. There certainly hadn't been anything else to recommend the story. Profiling someone who studied the agonizingly slow growth of coral sure as hell wasn't up his alley. Way too boring.

He looked around for signs of life. Nothing. Great. The last thing he wanted to do was sit out in this heat for the next hour. Then again, he didn't see an air-conditioning unit attached to the house, which meant it would be just as hot inside as out. Double great. He turned back to the door and knocked again, this time loud enough to raise the dead.

"Hello." A woman's holler wafted through the thick Florida air.

He looked around but didn't see anyone. Where had that voice come from?

"Out here."

This time he pinpointed the direction of the sound. Shading his eyes, he looked out to sea. Bobbing in the waves not too far from shore, someone waved. Laura Evans, no doubt.

"Hang on. I'll be right in." The woman headed toward shore, her crawl stroke strong and sure.

Austin stepped off the porch and headed to the shoreline, trying not to think of the misery that stretched out before him. Two weeks of heat and humidity. Two weeks of listening to facts guaranteed to put even the dullest of readers to sleep. Two weeks of being stuck in a tiny house with some homely academic whose personality was probably as dull as the subject she studied. "Caleb, old buddy, you're a dead man."

Breathing in the tangy salt air, he watched Laura swim up to the rocky shoreline.

She swam to the rocks and grabbed hold of a metal handle that had been fixed to the rough surface. "Let me get my fins off and I'll be right out." Her mask gave the words a nasal tone as she reached beneath the water with her free hand.

He cocked a brow in surprise at the two lovely sun-kissed shoulders bobbing above the water. His subject was only thirty, but still, considering her occupation, he'd expected her skin to be deeply brown and tanned to a tough hardness by the sun. And he'd expected her frame to be more masculine than feminine, like many of the women he'd met who were into extreme sports or occupations normally occupied by men.

But the shoulders he was staring at now were none of those things. They were strong, yes. But there wasn't a damned masculine thing about them. And the skin covering them—soft, resilient and golden— begged for a man's touch. Maybe, just maybe, the next couple of weeks wouldn't be a complete bore after all.

He looked back to her face, trying to get a glimpse of her features, wondering if her face was as beautiful as her shoulders. Unfortunately, her mask distorted what few features it didn't obscure.

With a splash of water she pulled a bright pink flipper out of the ocean and set it on one of the rock's flat surfaces. The second flipper followed shortly after. Then she grabbed the metal handle and pulled herself from the waves. Water sluiced down her body, exposing two of the most luscious breasts he'd ever seen.

He swallowed hard, his gaze following the water's downward path. A tiny waist. Softly curved hips. Looong, sculpted legs. And all that beautiful, golden-hued skin set off to mouthwatering perfection by her white one-piece bathing suit.

Wow.

He pulled his gaze from her gorgeous body just as she snapped her mask off.

Big hazel doe eyes. A cute little nose that turned up at the end. High, wide cheekbones. And bee-stung lips that sent sweat sliding down his spine just thinking about what they'd be good for.

Better than wow.

Double wow.

Caleb, old buddy, you've just gotten a reprieve.

Oh, jeez. The man was early.

Laura Evans stepped toward the tall figure standing by the shore's edge, doing her best to not look disconcerted. She'd fully intended to be dressed in a business suit all nice and neat and professional when he arrived. It was important she appear professional. Important the man take her seriously. Something her family's wealth made much more difficult than it should be. Well, her family's wealth and certain physical attributes she couldn't do anything about.

And if the man's focus meant anything—or the purely male turn of his lips—he was already being sidetracked by the top-heavy part of her body. Sheesh. What was it with men and their fascination with breasts? Just once she'd like a man to look at her and see her brains. Or her heart. But no, their eyes always went straight to her chest.

She put a smile on her face and cleared her throat, hoping to bring his attention up a notch or two. "Good afternoon."

He raised his gaze, his green eyes sparkling with easy charm. "Afternoon. Laura Evans, I presume?"

He was tall, dark, broad-shouldered. Handsome in a rugged, "let's do Mount Everest" kind of way. But it wasn't his looks that snagged her attention. It was his presence. He vibrated with self-confidence and energy and pure, raw maleness. And that easy charm was an interesting combination with the rugged facade.

She held out her hand, letting the water dripping from her fingers speak for itself. "I'd shake your hand, but…"

He took it anyway, enclosing it in his big, strong

grip. "No problem. A little water never hurt anyone. Nice to meet you, Laura Evans. I'm Austin Brady from *Land, Sea & Sky Magazine*."

Heat and electricity engulfed her hand. And galloped up her arm with surprising intensity. Amazing. It was just a handshake, for pity's sake; she should have barely noticed his touch.

But she noticed it. The hot little tingles shooting through her system and collecting in her belly were impossible to ignore. She wasn't at all sure what that reaction meant, but she was pretty sure it wasn't good. Not for a thirty-year-old virgin bent on staying that way.

But the unexpected heat racing through her wasn't her only concern. Who was this guy? "I'm sorry, did you say your name was Brady? I was expecting Dean Michaels."

The man grimaced. "I take it Caleb Jacobs never got a hold of you to tell you Michaels isn't coming." He shook his head. "There'll be payback for that. I hate disappointing a beautiful lady. Unfortunately, Caleb wanted Dean on the new volcano erupting in the Pacific. So he sent me instead."

Oh no, she'd been looking forward to meeting Michaels. Not only was the man the best underwater photographer in the business, but he had several science degrees, one of them in marine biology. And he cared about the environment. His articles always underscored how important it was to stop destroying the earth they lived on and start nurturing it. He was the perfect journalist for this article.

She took a deep, calming breath. She wasn't going to panic yet. She'd get Mr. Brady up to the house and diplomatically grill him on his credentials. Maybe he was as qualified as Michaels. Maybe he was just as good with a camera. God, she hoped so. This article was important to the reefs. Important to her.

She waved a hand toward her house. "Why don't we go on up to the house? I'll show you where you're sleeping and then I can change while you bring in your bags and equipment."

The corner of his mouth twitched. "Don't change on my account. This is an informal interview. What you're wearing is fine. Perfect, in fact."

With many men the comment would have offended her. But his eyes sparkled with mischief, not lascivious intent. And his smile was so full of boyish charm, it was impossible to take exception. But she didn't want anything interfering with this article, least of all sexual tension. She shook her head and chuckled. "I think I'd be more comfortable in something a little drier. Come on." She struck out for the house.

He fell in beside her. "So, I take it you do live here?"

She caught the note of disappointment in the casual query. He was doing his best to hide it, but she heard it. Her stomach sank a notch as she realized what it meant. She winced. "I take it my quaint little domicile isn't exactly what you were expecting?"

A hint of a smile tugged at his lips. "Considering your family connections, no."

She sighed. "So, you know who my family is, huh?"

"Oh yeah, the Evanses of Evans Yachts fame—the leading manufacturers of racing yachts and sports boats in the world. A family that is mentioned as often in the financial section of the paper as they are in the sports section. I'd be a pretty sad reporter if I missed such a significant connection. Particularly since your brother Seth was in the news not so long ago with his boat exploding."

Yes, the exploding boat. She wished she knew what had really gone on there. The explosion had been reported to the press as an accident. A malfunction in the engine. That was what Laura's parents and big brother had told her, too. But she didn't believe it.

There'd been too many "accidents" happening around her family lately for her to believe it. But, as usual, no one was talking to her. Her father had rallied the family to keep her out of the loop. Frustrating and worrisome. She didn't like the thought of her family being in danger and not letting her help in some way. But there didn't seem to be anything she could do about it. And right now she needed to concentrate on Austin Brady and her article.

"The boat explosion was an unfortunate accident.

And I suppose you would be a sorry reporter if you'd missed the family connection." But she had hoped and she couldn't quite keep the frustration from her voice.

He cocked his head, studying her. "Is there a family feud I missed in my quick research? Are you estranged from your family?"

She shook her head. "Not at all. And you would have discovered who my family was sooner or later." She grimaced. "Sooner actually, as we've been invited for—interpret that as commanded to appear for—dinner tomorrow night. But I was hoping to get through the initial introductions as just Laura Evans, marine biologist. I didn't want whatever reporter Caleb sent to assume I was some little rich girl playing at a job."

His lips twitched, just enough to let her know the thought had indeed crossed his mind.

She sighed. "I see I'll just have to work harder to dispel that image. Although—" she smiled wickedly "—my humble little house should help." She climbed her steps and opened her door, waving him in.

He walked past her into the house, his gaze sweeping over the small living room/kitchen combination.

She stared at his broad back, a nervous frisson running over her. While her abode might well dispel his image of her as a spoiled rich girl, she was afraid it might irritate him as well. He'd obviously come here expecting to find a big, fancy house with *all* the amenities. Her place was comfortable and tidy, but it was definitely not fancy. And it was dismally short on the amenities. "Big disappointment?" she asked, holding her breath and praying he didn't mind the simpler accommodations.

He turned to her with an easy, downright sexy smile. "Sharing close quarters with such a lovely lady? Never."

Those tingles kicked up again. Stronger this time. Hotter. Not good. This was definitely *not* the direction she wanted this relationship to take. Maybe, if she covered up, he'd quit looking at her like… like…well, like she was some delicious treat set out just for his enjoyment.

She snatched a beach towel from the big rack of them she kept near the entrance and wrapped it around herself, ignoring the telltale flush she knew was coloring her skin. "I'm glad you're not too disappointed, because, while I love my parents dearly, we definitely have a difference of opinion on lifestyles. I like the simple life. Like living on the salary I earn." She waved a hand toward the sofa. "Your bed. Not fancy, but I've slept there often enough to assure you it's quite comfortable."

He tipped a shoulder. "I'm sure it will be fine."

A moment of awkward silence fell. At least it seemed awkward to her. He, on the other hand, seemed content to stand there, smiling, watching her. Which was *not* helping those disturbing tingles go away.

Professional, she reminded herself. She wanted to present a professional front. Not easy to do in a beach towel, but she'd do the best she could. She pulled herself up to her full height and cleared her throat, forcing her mind to the business at hand. "So, Mr. Brady, have you been writing for *Land, Sea & Sky Magazine* long?"

His lips twitched. "You're not really going to call me Mr. Brady, are you?"

"Yeah, actually, I am. I think keeping this on a professional level is the best thing we can do."

He laughed, his eyes twinkling with humor. "If you want to give that a try, I'm all for it."

Okay, so he thought they couldn't do it. With the heat sliding through her she wasn't so sure, either. But she was definitely going to try. And let's face it, she was a pro at keeping men at bay. She'd done it for thirty years. Not because she didn't like men. She did. But because she'd yet to find a man who liked her more than he liked her bank account—or her family's business.

And a long time ago she'd decided not to settle for being second on any man's list of wants.

Of course, her biggest weapon for keeping men at bay in the past had always been her job—she'd be dragging Mr. Brady to work with her for the next few weeks. And no other man had affected her in quite this tummy-tingling way. But...

That was no doubt a temporary aberration. One that would subside once they were around each other more. And tummy tingles or not, this was a matter she couldn't afford to lose her concentration on. She pulled her shoulders back another inch and concentrated on the task at hand—Mr. Brady's credentials. "So, how long have you been writing for *Land, Sea & Sky*?"

He shook his head, that sexy humor still sparkling in his eyes. "I'm freelance, actually. But Caleb and I are old buddies. So when the eruption took his writer and he needed another journalist quick, he gave me a call. Talked me into it."

Freelance? Talked him into it? That didn't sound good. She strode away from him, out of the small entrance and into her living room, where she could put some distance between them. "I hope he didn't have to twist your arm too hard."

"I owe Caleb too many favors for him to have to twist too hard."

Which was great for Caleb. But she wasn't so sure it was good for her. Had Mr. Brady taken the job *only* because he'd owed his buddy a favor? Or because he owed the magazine editor a favor *and* the article was right up his alley of expertise? There was only one way to find out. "What magazines have you written for in the past?"

He shrugged, those big shoulders moving fluidly under the casual cotton of his shirt. "*Time, Newsweek, Sports Afield, Smithsonian* and several others."

All top-of-the-line magazines. The knot in her chest eased a bit. The guy could obviously write. But none of those magazines was a science journal. "That's an impressive list, but it's a pretty diverse bunch. It doesn't tell me much about what you like to write. What are your favorite kinds of stories?" She held her breath, praying he had a list of science or nature articles to his name.

"I like anything that offers a spark of excitement, but I think I like the war stories the best. They have everything. Life-and-death conflict. Emotional and political importance. And while I collect the facts, there's nothing like dodging bullets to get the adrenaline pumping. Although I did an article on smoke jumpers last year that was a damned close second. Jumping out of planes and hoping you don't land in a wall of flames gets your heart pumping pretty good, too. And I've done a few articles on extreme sports that were exciting."

Oh, God. A thrill seeker. She swallowed hard, the knot in her chest almost strangling her. How would a thrill-seeking adrenaline junkie ever understand the delicate balance between her reefs and the fish that inhabited them? "Have you ever done any science articles?"

He shook his head. "This is my first. Science isn't really my strong point."

Not his strong point? Dread washed through her. This was not good. As he'd pointed out, her family was featured in the paper and in magazines all the time. She'd seen firsthand how reporters who didn't know anything about the subject they were reporting on screwed up the facts. "Do you know anything about reefs? Anything about the ocean?"

His lips twisted wryly. "Not a bit. But don't let it worry you. We'll manage."

Science wasn't his strong point. He had *no* knowledge of the reefs *or* the ocean? But they'd *manage.* How did he figure?

Maybe she could call the magazine, get them to send another reporter. Yeah, right. They'd gone outside their sources to find Brady. Obviously they didn't have any extra reporters hanging around. And if she requested a change, the next reporter they sent might not have Brady's qualifications. She would have to manage.

Frustration pounded through her.

She didn't want to just *manage.* She wanted— *needed*—this article to be wonderful. But how was she going to pull that off with a man who didn't know the first thing about the ocean? The first thing about the delicate balance between nature and man? How was she going to pull it off with a man who got his thrills reporting on death and destruction?

Two

A few minutes later Laura stood in her bedroom in front of her open closet in her wet swimsuit, thankful for what little coolness the wet material provided. With her bedroom door closed, the room was like an overheated sauna, making it hard to breathe and even harder to think.

She usually threw open all the doors and windows, letting the almost continual breeze off the Gulf cool the place. But as long as Aus—*Mr. Brady* was sitting in her living room she couldn't very well leave her bedroom door open while she changed. And she needed to get out of this wet swimsuit and into something dry and businesslike to get this meeting onto a professional track.

She grabbed the black silk pants and white silk blouse she'd chosen for their initial meeting and tossed them on the bed. Putting on the long pants and long-sleeved shirt held about as much appeal as slipping into a cauldron of boiling water. The only consolation was that once she got dressed she wouldn't have to be in this suffocating room any longer. Or even in her house for long.

Previously, she'd suggested they head over to one

of the local restaurants for an early drink and dinner. A suggestion Brady had jumped on immediately as he'd sat on her couch and all but melting into the cushions.

That nervous little knot in her chest tightened again. While Dean Michaels would have understood her lack of air-conditioning, even heartily approved of it, she didn't think Brady found it anything but uncomfortable—and inconvenient. The sooner she got him to a cool place, the better.

As she stripped off her swimsuit and toweled dry, beads of sweat popped right back out on her skin. Terrific. By the time she left this room she would look like a sweaty, rumpled rat. Man, she wished she could open the door, let a little air in.

But while she was comfortable with the notion of just telling the man to look somewhere else while she dressed, she didn't think he would take the instruction quite so casually. And the last thing she needed was to titillate the sexual tension already crackling between them. So she ignored how the clothes clung to her damp skin and desperately tried to come up with a way to make this article work.

Obviously, Brady preferred a different kind of story. But maybe Caleb Jacobs had sent him because his photography was so exceptional. Maybe Caleb thought the man's talents with a camera would compensate for his lack of knowledge and enthusiasm for the subject. A man probably didn't have to know anything about a subject to take superb photos. And wasn't a picture supposed to be worth a thousand words?

A little thread of hope wound through her. If done properly, pictures *could* tell the story. She couldn't imagine anyone looking at a picture of a vibrant, healthy reef and comparing it to a picture of a dead one without understanding the reef's plight. Of course, convincing them the reef's troubles were a warning sign that man had better start taking care of the planet might be a little trickier with photos. But she could work with it.

Now all she had to do was find out if Brady had enough talent with a camera to pull it off. She dabbed on a bit of perfume, grabbed the suit jacket from the closet and strode out of the stifling room.

Brady's gaze swept over her the minute she walked out the door. An amused smiled turned his lips, as if he knew how hard she was trying to put a professional barrier between them.

Well, let him smile. He might be used to women falling into his bed, but she'd practically made a career of *not* falling into men's beds. And she didn't intend to change that habit now. No matter how much her tummy tingled. She tipped her head toward the front door in a very businesslike manner. "Let's head on over to the restaurant."

He followed her out with that fight-it-all-you-want-but-you're-still-mine smile turning his lips.

Shaking her head, she strode toward her car and opened the driver's door.

He stopped in his tracks, the smile disappearing, his brows pulling low as he stared at her car. He quickly waved a hand toward his rental. "Tell you what, let's take my car."

She laughed, dropping into the driver's seat. "Relax. Mine has air-conditioning, too. I'll even turn it on for you."

His shoulders slumped with relief and he jogged around to the passenger side and slid into the bucket seat next to her.

She tried not to notice how close he was. How the heat of his shoulder soaked into hers. How his butter-soft jeans clung to his long thighs and cupped the intriguing masculine bulge below his belt. Oh, man. She jerked her gaze away before she was caught, and forced her mind to the problem at hand. After all, the man's sexiness wasn't going to get her article written! In fact, she couldn't see it getting her anything but flat out trouble.

She turned the ignition and flicked on the air-conditioning. She could use a blast of icy air about now. Resolutely fixing her gaze out the windshield, she pulled out of her drive. "So, Mr. Brady, when did you discover you liked taking pictures?" That was what she needed to concentrate on—his talent with a camera, not the fit of his jeans.

His lips twisted wryly. "I started taking pictures when someone offered to pay me to take a few."

"Really? When was that?"

He shot her a sideways glance. "Laura, if you're

looking for an edifying story to convince yourself I'm a competent photographer—and I suspect you are—this isn't the story you want to hear.''

Oh jeez, had she been that obvious? The last thing she wanted to do was insult the guy. Not only did he hold the success or failure of her article in his hands. But she suspected the only reason he was here was to do a favor for a friend. It wasn't his fault he didn't have the desired background for this article.

She did her best to look innocent. ''What on earth makes you think I'm questioning your ability? I'm sure you'll do a wonderful job on the story.''

He shook his head, his green eyes sparkling with laughter. ''You are such a bad liar.''

Heat scalded her cheeks. She *was* a bad liar. She sighed. ''Sorry. I didn't mean to offend you.''

''Don't worry about it. You're not the first person to inquire after my credentials, and I'm sure you won't be the last. I know you're worried about the article because I don't have a science background. But the article is going to be fine. And you needn't worry about the photos, either. Mine have won several awards.'' He shot her an easy smile. ''Feel better?''

''Yeah,'' she admitted sheepishly, the tension in her chest easing considerably. If the pictures were good, the article could be very powerful. And he obviously took great pictures. With that big worry behind her, curiosity took hold. ''How old *were* you when someone offered to pay you to take those first pictures?''

He shot her a droll look. "I'm warning you, this story doesn't get any better just because the end result is a few awards."

She shrugged. "Tell me, anyway." She wanted to know more about the man sitting next to her. Not perhaps the wisest impulse to give in to. She was pretty sure the more distance she kept between them the better. But since she'd be spending the next couple weeks with him, it would be nice to know something about him.

He grimaced. "Why don't I pick a more interesting story. I could tell you about the time I snowboarded from a helicopter in the Chugach Mountains."

She definitely didn't want to hear about some adrenaline high. Besides, his reluctance to tell the story just made her want to hear it more. "You can tell me about the Dew-boys' stunt later. Right now I want to hear about the first pictures." A sudden thought struck. "Wait a minute. What kind of pictures were they?"

He chuckled, low and sexy. "Not those kind."

"Whew." She mopped a hand across her brow, studiously ignoring the fresh wave of tingles his chuckle created. "Cough it up, then. How old were you?"

"Sixteen."

"Really? That's young. Had someone seen some

of your photos and liked your work?'' Had he been
a natural with a camera, a talent that had been des-
tined to come to light right from the beginning? A
little more tension eased from her chest.

He shook his head, that wry smile turning his lips
again. ''Nothing that dramatic, I'm afraid. I didn't
know anything about taking pictures at the time. I'd
never taken one in my life.''

Her brows shot up in surprise. ''So why did someone ask you to take some?''

''Because he figured an article on white-water rafting would be interesting, and he had space to fill in
the local paper.''

''So what? He grabbed some kid off the street,
which just happened to be you, shoved a camera in
your hands and told you to go rafting and shoot him
a few pictures?''

He smiled. ''Not quite. It was my junior year in
high school, and I was in a local bar with a bunch
of my buddies. We were sucking down sodas we'd
spiked in the bathroom with a bottle of smuggled-in
whiskey.''

She rolled her eyes. ''Smuggled-in booze. That
sounds like something my brothers would have done.
What is it about a teenage boy's psyche and whiskey? The minute their voices start to change they
reach for a bottle. Do they think it makes them look
older or something? More macho?''

He laughed. ''It's a guy thing. You'd never understand.''

"No kidding. I still don't understand why my brothers do half the things they do. So, on with the story. You and your delinquent cohorts were drinking spiked sodas and…"

"And playing pool while we talked about the white-water rafting trip we were heading out on the next day when an editor from the local paper came over to us. He said if one of us would take a camera, take some pictures, put a few words with them, he'd buy the story for twenty-five bucks and run the article in the paper."

"And you were the one who took the camera." It was more a statement than a question.

He shrugged. "The other guys came from upper-middle-class backgrounds. They thought having to drag the camera along wasn't worth the hassle. Not for twenty-five bucks. And I can see their point. Most of them got more than that every week for allowance. But for me, twenty-five bucks meant me and my mom could have hamburger in our mac and cheese for the next week."

So, he'd been poor. And he'd hadn't mentioned a father. Had the man died, leaving Brady and his mother alone to fend for themselves? Or was there another explanation for the father's absence? Those questions and others pounded at her brain. But they were sensitive questions, and the last thing she wanted to do was make him angry or uncomfortable with her. So she stuck to safe ground. "Were the pictures good?"

"Terrible. But the old man bought them and printed the story. I couldn't believe it. Getting paid to take pictures and write a few words about something I would have done anyway. And seeing my name on the story in the paper was a kick."

"I'll bet it was. Did you do more stories for him?"

"Absolutely. I liked hamburger in my mac and cheese. And later, when I headed to college, having done some pieces for the local paper made it easier for me to get on a bigger paper as a stringer. As time went on, the pictures got better, the words more fluent, my articles bigger. Once I finished college I realized photojournalism was the perfect occupation for me. I liked to travel. I liked adventure. I liked chasing that next big rush. And photojournalism allowed me to do those things and get paid for it."

"So what makes you think that isn't an edifying story?"

He shot her a droll look. "Come on, a man likes to create his own destiny, not just trip into it."

Another macho thing. She laughed softly. "Oh, I don't know. I think a lot of credit should go to someone who falls into something and is astute enough to realize it's where he belongs."

He tipped a shoulder. "Maybe. Either way, it's been a good living. Not only does it pay well, it's fun."

"That's the important thing. I firmly believe one should enjoy his work." That was why she was working at the Marine Institute instead of Evans

Yachts. And thinking of the institute sent her curiosity in another direction. "So when did you start diving?"

He looked at her in surprise. "Diving? I don't dive."

Shock skittered through her. "You don't?"

He shook his head.

"How do you take underwater pictures?"

He shrugged those big, sexy shoulders. "Actually, I never have before."

"What?" Her heart pounded in alarm.

"I've never taken underwater pictures before."

"You've never taken underwater pictures?" Had she thought her article was safe?

He chuckled. "Don't look so worried. Taking pictures is all in the eye. And I have a great eye."

"That may well be, but if you can't get down to where the pictures *are*, what good is your eye?" She couldn't keep the panic from her voice.

"Relax. I snorkel. I can do this article with both hands tied behind my back. Remember, I'm used to taking pictures with bullets and flames coming my way. This article will be a cinch."

Both hands tied behind his back?

A cinch?

The only thing more alarming than his lack of knowledge and ability to do this article was his lackadaisical attitude about it all.

A lot of the reefs where she would need him to take pictures were a hundred feet down. And he thought he could take them with both hands tied behind his back while he snorkeled?

Her article was doomed.

Austin got out of the car at the restaurant and headed around to open Laura's door. Before he'd even rounded the end of the car she opened her own door and let herself out. A small smile pulled at his lips. She was doing everything in her power to keep this evening on a business level.

He'd almost laughed when she'd come out of her bedroom. It was a hundred and fifty degrees out, for crying out loud, and she'd put on long black pants and a long-sleeved shirt—and thrown a suit jacket over her shoulder for good measure. He'd wanted to ask her why she hadn't just donned on a suit of armor and a chastity belt while she was at it. But he'd refrained. Because her all-business attitude had an almost innocent appeal to it. And because he knew her efforts were futile.

He'd never felt such crackling electricity between himself and a woman before. And there was no doubt in his mind she felt it, too. She could put on all the clothes she wanted and cling to her illusive cloak of professionalism until her fingers turned blue, but sooner or later they were going to end up together, skin to skin. The only question was, how soon.

He grimaced. It might have been a lot sooner if he hadn't screwed up on the way over here. Unfortunately, saying he could do this article with his hands tied behind his back had not produced the result he'd anticipated. He wasn't sure why his words hadn't reassured her that her article was in safe hands. Particularly since he *could* do this article with his hands tied behind his back. His hands tied behind his back, both legs chopped off and blindfolded. But his comment had only upset her.

In fact she'd looked—still looked—as if he'd sentenced her to stand in front of a firing squad at dawn. He fell into step beside her as they made their way to the restaurant, wondering what he could say that would make her feel better. But as he pulled the heavy door open for her, he decided against saying anything. After all, it was his last bit of reassurance that had gotten him into this mess. And...

He was good at what he did, dang it. He didn't have to prove himself to her. When the article was finished, she'd see that she'd had nothing to worry about in the first place. Besides, he didn't want to spend the night wrangling over the article. Not when there was something so much more interesting to concentrate on.

Something like Laura Evans.

She was the most interesting thing he'd run across in a long time. With her sitting across the table from him the last thing he wanted to hear about was coral and fish. He wanted to know about Laura. He wanted to know what she liked to eat, what kind of music she liked to listen to, what made her laugh. Of course, he was going to have to shift subjects subtly.

She was pretty set on this let's-keep-it-professional thing. If he wasn't careful she might well drop-kick him out of the restaurant. But he could be subtle. No problem.

He followed Laura and the maître d' to a well lit area where tables clustered around a noisy, spewing fountain. "How's this?" the young man asked.

Austin glanced around, quickly finding what he was looking for. He pointed to a table in a dark, secluded corner. "How about that table over there?"

The maître d' nodded with a knowing wink. "No problem."

Laura cataloged the wink, took one look at the table in the corner and shook her head. "Oh, no. This will be fine." She started to pull out the chair in front of her.

Austin quickly took her elbow, keeping her on her feet. "No, this will never do. The fountain is too hard to hear over and once the dinner crowd arrives, it's going to be too noisy to talk here. Come on, let's sit over here where I'll be able to hear about the reefs." He gently but surely led her toward the intimate table, patting himself on the back for that last bit of genius. How could she possibly object when he claimed his reason for the quiet table centered around business?

Of course, if the scowl she tossed him was any indication, he wasn't fooling her a bit. But she didn't fight him. She let him lead her to the shadowed corner, either because she didn't want to make a scene or because she was just too nice to outwardly object. Either way, he took full advantage, seating her at the small table and taking the chair across from her.

The maître d' laid their menus down and took their drink orders.

Austin slipped the guy a five, gave him a thanks-brother smile and turned his attention to Laura. The corner was heavily shadowed, allowing the candle-light to give off a golden glow. A glow that brought out the amber in her hazel eyes and glistened off the clear gloss that made her lips look wet and swollen and thoroughly kissable. Heat shot through him just thinking about tasting those lips.

And having them taste him.

He swallowed hard and shoved that thought away. He was getting way ahead of himself. He picked up his menu and forced his mind to focus on the words printed on the page instead of the erotic thoughts pounding in his brain. "What—" He cleared the gravel from his throat and tried again. "What do you recommend?"

"All their food is excellent."

"Yeah? What do you like to eat?" He spied fresh, live lobster halfway down the menu. That sounded good. Almost good enough to get his mind off the pounding in his groin.

Almost.

Laura opened her menu and started to peruse the items. "I like anything that doesn't come out of the sea."

"Really?" How odd for someone who'd been raised on the coast. "No crab or lobster or sushi, even?"

She shrugged. "You might talk me into a little rice and cucumber wrapped in seaweed. But crab or lobster? No way. I don't eat my friends."

Uh-oh. He snapped his gaze up. "How do you feel about those around you eating them?"

"I don't pawn my beliefs off on others. Feel free to eat what you like."

He thought she meant it. But if she didn't eat her friends he didn't think she'd be thrilled to watch him eat them, either. He raised a worried brow. "How do you feel about people eating cow?"

She smiled, obviously relieved. "Since I don't know any personally—and since they're not being eaten faster than they're reproducing—it doesn't bother me a bit."

Well, he could be thankful for that. After his faux pas in the car he didn't want anything else creating distance between them. But he'd be damned if he'd spend the evening munching on rabbit food.

He leaned back in his chair, studying the woman across from him. A bit of her smile still lingered, a welcome change from the look of doom she'd worn into the restaurant. She was obviously willing to let the comment that had upset her in the car slip into the past. She got extra points for that. He knew a lot of women, particularly wealthy women, who held on to their hurt or anger until they'd beaten the offending mortal into the ground with it. Laura Evans obviously wasn't into holding grudges.

Imagine that. Beautiful. Sexy. And nice. An intriguing combination. One that made him want to know even more about her. He set his menu down and focused all his attention on her. "Okay, I now know you don't eat seafood. What else can you tell me about yourself?"

She set her menu down and gave him a sideways look. "I thought we were going to talk about the reefs?"

Not if he could help it. "We are. Eventually. But the article is actually a profile on you."

"Caleb said the profile angle is just to pull people in. That the main thrust of the article will be the reefs."

"Yep, that's the way it's done. I won't need your whole life history." Though he wouldn't mind knowing it. "But if I don't have a few facts, what am I going to draw the reader in with?"

She grimaced. "You already know the biggest fact about me. The one that will probably draw the readers in the best."

"Who your family is?"

She nodded. "Are you going to use it?"

She tried to sound nonchalant, but he heard her reluctance to have that information mentioned in the article. He'd definitely make points if he told her he wouldn't use it. But he made his living by writing good articles. Damned good articles. He considered this story a bit of a fluff piece, but that didn't mean he intended to write a sloppy story. "You have to admit it would be a big draw."

"Yeah, it would be. But I would rather you didn't use it."

He thought about the conversation they'd had in her yard. "You're afraid people won't take your research seriously?"

"Yes."

"I would think if the research is valid, it will speak for itself."

"The research is valid," she stated emphatically. "But you have to admit that my background has the potential to color the readers' thoughts. If they think I'm some rich girl just playing at my job, what's to say they won't think my data is bogus? That I collected it here and there between trips around the world and then shoved it into some theory just to make myself sound important?"

"Maybe." He thought for a moment. "I'm sure Caleb knows who your family is. Did he agree not to use that tidbit?"

"We talked about it. He thought it would be a good draw, too. But he also understood my viewpoint. In the end, he said he'd leave it up to the reporter doing the story."

Gee, thanks, old buddy. Let me be the bad guy; "I'll tell you what. If I can find a way to make the article just as strong without it, I'll leave it out. Otherwise, it goes in. Deal?"

Her smile was back, full force. "Deal." She stuck out her hand.

He shook it, enjoying the feel of her soft skin and the electricity that arced between them before leaning back in his chair. "Okay, then, tell me something about yourself that's as powerful a lure as your family name."

The waiter arrived with their drinks, and she took a sip of her kir. "Let's see. I graduated from the University of South Florida with honors when I was twenty-one and received my master's in marine biology when I was twenty-three. I never went for my doctorate. I was so involved with research by then and I didn't want to lose any time to course work." She wrinkled her nose. "Do you think the readers will hold that against me?"

He chuckled at her earnestness. "No. I'm sure a master's degree will give you plenty of credibility. But while the reader will want to know your education history, it's not the kind of thing that will reel the reader in. Tell me something about *you.* Something about Laura Evans."

She looked a little stumped. "Like what?"

He thought for a second, sifting through the myriad things *he* wanted to know about her. "What's your favorite color?"

"My favorite color? No reader is going to care about that."

"Actually, personal likes and dislikes are usually a good way to catch a reader's eye. Details make the subject of the article human. Turn him or her into the guy next door.''

Her look turned skeptical. ''I could see readers wanting to know what my favorite fish in the ocean is. But no one is going to care what my favorite color is. That sounds like a dating question to me.'' She shot him an admonishing look. ''The kind of question a man who is interested in a lady would ask.''

He just smiled. ''You're right, it might well be the type of question a man who is interested in a woman might ask. But I also think it has value for the article.''

She gave him a look that clearly said he was full of bull.

He smiled, took a lazy sip of his bourbon and kept his gaze expectantly on hers, waiting for her answer.

She drummed her fingers on the table, watching him, no doubt waiting for him to give up and ask another question.

He took a tight hold on the smile threatening to break loose and took another slow sip of his drink. ''Come on, Laura, tell the readers.''

A short burst of sound escaped her lips, half laughter, half exasperation. Then her expression turned thoughtful. Way too thoughtful for someone merely trying to select her favorite color.

Suddenly she smiled, a smile that leaned far more toward pitchforks and tails than wings and halos. ''You may tell your readers my favorite color is whatever color the ocean is when I'm standing in front of it.''

The little devil. She'd answered the question, all right, possibly even with a certain amount of honesty. But it hadn't been a personal answer. It had been an answer designed to give him an interesting reply to put in print *and* keep the focus of the conversation on the ocean, not on her. An answer designed to keep him from discovering anything truly personal about her.

He chuckled. "Good. Very good.''

She gave him a smug nod. "I thought so. And if these answers are for your article how come you're not writing them down?''

"Because I'm used to remembering. It's pretty hard to stop in the middle of a battlefield or an extreme sport and write something down. Now—''

He thought carefully about his next question, looking for one she couldn't turn back toward her profession. "How about music? What's your favorite type of music? Country and western? Rock and roll? Heavy metal?'' Let her find a way to hook that to the great blue.

Her brow wrinkled in thought.

Yeah, he had her.

But then that impish smile was back and her hazel eyes sparkled with humor. "Actually, I like a lot of music. But one of my favorite tapes is of humpback whales talking to each other. Their sounds are so sweet and sad and gentle. It has to be some of the most beautiful music on earth.''

Wow. She *was* good. Very good. But he was better. He had a question she couldn't possibly turn around. One he'd been wondering about since she'd stepped out of her bedroom dressed in her professional suit of armor—and smelling like heaven. Providing heaven smelled like every man's fantasy of the perfect woman. Sensuously sweet. Provokingly spicy. With a heady undercurrent of erotic musk. He drew in a deep breath, savoring the scent wafting across the table even now, and then asked, ''What's your favorite perfume?''

The humor in her eyes turned to pure triumph. ''Ocean Dreams,'' she quipped, smiling from ear to ear.

He snapped back in his chair. ''Liar.''

She shook her head and laughed, the sound clear and easy. ''No, I'm not. It's made by Giorgio.''

''You are making that up.''

She shook her head again. ''I'll show you the bottle when we get home.''

Blood shot straight to his groin. *When we get home.* Intimate words. They didn't mean anything. Yet. But he had every intention they would.

Soon.

Very soon. Because nothing got his blood pumping better than a good challenge.

And Laura Evans was going to be one fun, exciting, mind-blowingly sexy challenge.

Three

Laura lay in her bed that night, trying to ignore the sweat covering her body and the fact that the air was so hot it felt like she couldn't breathe. On hot nights she usually left her front and back doors open and slept on the sofa where the cross breeze would help keep her cool. But Brady was out there tonight. So she was stuck in here.

She'd thought briefly about collecting her blankets and bedding down on the living room floor where she knew at least some breeze blew. But she'd nixed the idea when she realized Brady might take it as an invitation.

And that she might let him.

She thought about him now, lying on her sofa, not more than twenty feet away. That big, hard, sexy body. It was a...disturbing thought. She turned over for the thousandth time and smiled at the ceiling. *Disturbing* was a good word. A safe word. Much safer than...tantalizing. Particularly since there wasn't anything more between them than those few feet.

She'd started the night out with her bedroom door closed, thinking a barrier between was a good idea.

But when she'd almost died of heatstroke, she'd sneaked over and opened it, hoping a stray breeze would find its way in. Ha! She might as well give up on catching any *Z's* tonight. It wasn't going to happen.

She flopped over again, trying to find a position that would alleviate the heat, trying to stop her mind from dwelling on her time at the restaurant with Brady. Another hopeless quest. She'd had fun tonight. More fun than she'd had in a long time. Way more than she should have had for someone trying to keep a relationship on a strictly professional basis.

She had somehow managed not to divulge any real personal data to Brady. At least not anything she didn't think belonged in the article. But his questions and her attempts to evade them had definitely turned into flirting. And she'd enjoyed every minute of it.

She sighed and turned over again, the heat compounding the restless energy snaking through her.

"Laura?" Brady's voice was quiet, tentative, as if he wasn't sure she was awake.

She stilled, holding her breath. She wasn't at all sure letting him know she was awake was wise. She'd had trouble keeping a professional distance from the man at the secluded, but still very public table at the restaurant. In the privacy of her home, in the dark, while she was lying in her bed, she'd be best not to push her luck.

"Laura, are you awake in there?"

The question wasn't any louder than his last query.

He was still being careful not to wake her if she was asleep. But the second inquiry made her wonder if he needed something. Self-preservation told to her to just keep quiet, that there wasn't anything he couldn't live without until morning. But in the end, the hostess in her won out. "I'm awake, do you need anything?"

"Yeah, an air conditioner. You don't happen to have one stuck in a closet somewhere, do you?" There was a bit of little-boy whine in his voice.

She smiled. That was one of the things she liked best about him—the boyish quality that took the edge off his almost overpowering energy and his I-can-do-this-article-with-my-hands-tied-behind-my-back arrogance. "Sorry, not a one. They're not ecologically sound, you know. Do you know how much power it takes to air-condition a whole house? Depleting the ozone layer, global warming. Ring any bells?"

"Ah. That's why you don't have one. I'd wondered. At first I thought the place might just be a workstation, and the company you worked for didn't want to splurge for the amenity. Then when I found out it was your home, I wondered if it was economic. You mentioned you liked living on your salary."

She laughed. "Believe it or not, the institute pays well enough that its workers can afford air-conditioning."

There was a stretch of silence, then, "So I suppose it wouldn't do any good for me to offer to buy one and have it installed."

She chuckled. "Absolutely not."

Another stretch of silence.

"You know, a lot of people don't realize it, but the heat can actually kill people."

She laughed outright now. "*Old* people, Brady. And people with heart conditions. Somehow I don't think you fall into either of those categories."

"Hmm. I wonder if this kind of heat can *give* a person a heart condition."

She laughed again. "Oh, for pity's sake, suck it up. It's a lot hotter in here than it is out there. You don't hear me complaining, do you?"

"You think it's hotter in there?"

"Oh, yeah."

Silence.

"You could come out here. I'll make room for you on the couch."

She could hear the impish, sexy smile in his voice, see it in her mind's eye. She shook her head. "Are you hitting on me?"

"I've been hitting on you all night. Are you just now noticing?" That boyish whine was in full swing again.

And she loved it. Unfortunately, it was time to put a stop to this. "I've noticed. And I have to admit I've enjoyed it. But, Brady, you might as well know up front, it's a waste of your time."

"Hitting on a pretty girl is never a waste of time. Futile sometimes. But never a waste of time."

"Fine. Futile, then. Now go to sleep."

"You've got to be kidding. In this heat? Neither one of us is going to sleep, and you know it. We might as well talk. Tell me why you think it's futile."

Oh man, the guy never gave up. A certain part of his appeal. But one she *had* to resist. "I don't *think,* Brady. I know."

A plaintive sigh whispered through the dark. "Okay, you know. But I'm curious to know *why* you know it. 'Cause I got to tell you, the vibes I feel humming between us tell a very different story."

Didn't she know it. But she was an adult, long past the time when she would give in to her baser feelings. Actually, she'd *never* given in to them.

Maybe that was why they seemed so intense now.

Regardless, her policy hadn't changed. "I decided a long time ago to avoid jumping into bed with a man until I knew him. Really knew him."

"Well, that's easy to fix. What would you like to know?" The smile was back in his voice.

She shook her head, smiling in the dark. "A few questions aren't going to save you, Brady. I won't consider sleeping with a man until I've known him for months."

"Months?"

She laughed at the shock in his voice. "Yeah, months."

"Maybe we could negotiate that time limit."

She smiled. "I don't think so. It's there for a reason."

Another long sigh. "And that reason would be? Not that I'm knocking it, you understand," he quickly amended. "It's just that you must admit, in this day and age, that kind of time stipulation is a bit unusual."

She thought about that for a moment. "I suppose it is. But I have to wonder if more people employed it, or something like it, if there would be as many broken hearts around."

Silence.

"Did someone break your heart, Laura?" The question was quiet, serious.

She stared at the ceiling, the soft moonlight glinting off the far corner, thinking about the dating she'd done in her early twenties. About the men who had taught her wealth could have very definite drawbacks. "Not broken really. Cracked maybe."

"Recently?"

She shook her head then realized he couldn't see it. "No. Several years ago, actually."

"It must have been a big crack to make you so cautious."

"I think it was more a compound effect. The first guy cracked it a little, then the next guy came along and cracked it a little more, and then the next guy. I finally woke up one morning and said, 'Hey, I'm smarter than this.'"

"Smarter than what? Were you picking the wrong guys?"

She thought for a moment, debating whether or

not to continue this conversation. They were definitely getting onto personal ground here. On the other hand, maybe getting the reason for the time stipulation out in the open would be a good thing. Maybe he'd back off a little if he thought she had a valid reason.

A shaft of disappointment flashed through her. She liked his flirting. She would miss it. But like sweet desserts, it was undoubtedly best avoided. "Listen, I know this might sound a bit like a poor-little-rich-girl whine, but the guys who come knocking at my door never seem to be interested in me. I could be the stupidest, meanest, grossest human being alive and they wouldn't care. Because they're not after me. They're after my money or their very own Evans yacht. It's something that isn't always apparent right away. But give them a few months and their real wishes come to the surface."

A cricket chirped somewhere in the corner of the room.

He was silent so long she thought she might have made her case. But then his voice sounded in the darkness, quieter, more serious than before. "I don't do long-term relationships, Laura. There was a time in my life when I thought it might be nice. But I'm a realist. There's too much of my father in me for it to ever work. So you can rest easy. I have neither your money nor one of your family's yachts in my sights."

Was he telling her he could offer a risk-free relationship because he'd be leaving as soon as the article was finished? And if he was, was that a good thing or a bad thing? And was it the truth? She'd certainly heard more than one rendition of "I'm not after your money." She decided to probe deeper. "How are you like your father?"

"Let's just say itchy feet seem to run in my family. My dad could never stay in one place for more than a few weeks at a time. I seem to have the same problem. But unlike my old man, I don't think it's okay to leave a wife and kid behind while I practice my footloose-and-fancy-free life." He tried to make his voice light, but beneath the even words was an ocean of bitterness.

She'd wondered earlier why his dad had been absent from his childhood. Now she knew. The jerk had left Brady and his mother at home, eating macaroni and cheese while he traveled around the world. And Brady resented him for it. She could well believe he didn't intend to do the same. But...

"I'm sorry about your dad, Brady. And I applaud you for knowing that family life doesn't suit you or your lifestyle. But..." She injected a bit of dry humor in her voice to lighten the mood. "I'm not sure the fact that you don't believe in long-term relationships is the best reason for me to waive a policy designed to save my heart."

He laughed softly. "Well, maybe not. On the other hand, you said you didn't want to be involved with a man who wants your money or one of your family's boats. I don't want either. I just want you, Laura Evans. Just you.''

Heat and need poured through her. A need so sharp it hurt. But while she'd often lain awake nights dreaming of a man's touch, she'd also dreamed of finding a man who loved her. A man she could share life's ups and downs with. A man she could have a family and happily ever after with.

Brady was offering only the touching part of that dream. There wouldn't even be a chance for the sharing. Or holding tiny babies in her arms. Or happily ever after. ''I don't know, Brady. I've never pictured myself as a summer fling kind of gal.''

''Well, think about it. It would be short, yes. But short isn't necessarily bad. Actually, when you look back over your life, it usually comes to you not as one long, endless stream of happenings and events but as short, little vignettes. Your first day of school. The first time you rode a bike. Your sixteenth birthday. Your first kiss. It would be good between us, Laura. Nerve-shatteringly, mind-blowingly good. We'd have one hell of a memory to look back on.''

If the heat sliding through her or the tingles jingling in her tummy meant anything, yes, they would. But would it be enough? And what about the professional angle? If the affair went wrong, he could trash her article. Trash her one chance to make her family understand what she did at the institute. Trash *her*. In a very public forum.

''Laura?''

"Hmm?"

"Just...think about it." The words echoed through the dark, heated night.

The temp in the room kicked up another notch. Damn him, she *would* think about it. And think about it, and think about it.

And think about it.

Four

The next morning Austin sat in the passenger seat of Laura's car as they buzzed down the highway toward her office at the Florida Marine Research Institute's laboratory in Long Key. Last night had to have been the longest, most frustrating night of his life. Laura's house could not have been any cooler than the hottest corners in hell, making sleep impossible. Not that he would have been able to sleep, anyway. He'd been way too horny for that. But the heat had only added to the frustration.

He had the car's air-conditioning cranked to the max now, hoping to store enough cool in his system to make it through tonight. Hoping to cool down his still-overactive libido. Since he'd suggested Laura think about a short-term relationship, he hadn't been able to get out of his mind images of her curvy, naked body under his.

He cast a surreptitious glance at her now. She was so beautiful. Even in those hideous clothes. He wished he could crawl inside her head, see what she was thinking. She'd barely uttered a word since he'd suggested she think about a... What had she called it? A summer fling. He didn't know if the idea intrigued her or made her want to toss him out on his ear.

She leaned forward and twisted the air-conditioning knob down. "You're freezing me to death. You have to adjust your body's temperature gauge so you don't need this so much. It's bad for the atmosphere."

He shot her a sardonic look. "You know, they haven't actually proved that yet. And how can you possibly be cold? You're covered up from head to toe." When she'd first come out of her room dressed in another business suit, this one gray with a prim pink blouse, his day had taken a definite downturn.

She rolled her eyes. "Please tell me you're not one of those people who actually has to have the bullet hit him between the eyes before he'll admit that the crack of gunfire and the smoke in the air means someone's shooting. Global warming is real, buddy. And get over the clothes already."

He took in the no-nonsense, skin-covering suit once again. "How come you're not wearing a bathing suit? Or a wetsuit or something?"

She snorted. "Dream on. We're going to the office today. Not out to the ocean. Appropriate attire is required."

"There's appropriate and then there's ridiculously prim. I was hoping that after our talk last night you wouldn't feel you needed such barriers."

One delicate brow arched toward her hairline and a self-deprecating chuckle fell from her lips. "Are you kidding? After last night's discussion I'm wondering if I shouldn't go out and buy a chastity belt. For both of our sakes.''

''For both our sakes? Well, that's a good sign. At least I know you're thinking about what I said last night.'' His mood lightened considerably.

She pushed restless fingers through her hair. ''I'm thinking, Brady. But that doesn't mean you should hold your breath. And has it occurred to you that what I have on this morning might not have anything to do with you?''

Surprise zinged through him. ''Actually, that hadn't occurred to me. The fancy clothes aren't to keep me at bay?''

''I probably *should* have thought of that.'' Chagrin crossed her face. ''But my brain's not functioning all that well this morning. It's too tired.''

His, too. But her chastity-belt comment had perked him up. And now hearing she hadn't dressed to keep him at arm's length… ''So is that what you usually wear to work? Business suits?''

''Yeah.''

''Wow. Do the other field researchers wear suits, too?''

''No. A lot of them dress more casually. But then, they don't have to prove they're not just playing at a job.''

''Ah. The little-rich-girl syndrome again?''

She nodded.

"But you've worked at the institute for twelve years, right?"

She nodded, stifling a yawn. "Yep, since I was eighteen."

"Well, for crying out loud, haven't the people you work with figured out you're serious yet?"

She tipped a shoulder. "Most of them. But I worked way too hard convincing them of that to risk any backsliding. And putting on dress slacks instead of jeans isn't that big a deal."

Maybe not, but he'd sure prefer to see her in something else. But he was pretty sure saying so wouldn't win him any extra points, so he kept his mouth shut and moved to another subject. One he knew was close to her heart. "So what are we doing at your illustrious office today?"

"Illustrious it's not. But it is well supplied with the latest equipment—the only really important thing. I'm going to show you the computer program my team is creating. It's the heart of the project. It's not finished yet, but it's far enough along you'll be able to get an idea of what we're doing."

"Sounds good." Actually, a morning of computer programs and slow-growing coral sounded boring. But he had to collect the information sometime. And he wouldn't let the morning go to waste. He'd use the time to push Laura toward that yes he wanted so badly to hear.

She pulled into the lab's parking lot. "This is it.

The South Florida Regional Laboratory.'' She zipped into a parking space and got out.

He grabbed his camera and followed her, taking a quick glance around. ''It's bigger than I thought it would be.''

''It needs to be big. A lot of work goes on here.''

He raised the camera and clicked off several shots. Then he pointed to a big, lush bush in front of the white stucco. ''Go stand in front of that.''

She rolled her eyes but obliged, sticking her tongue out for the last shot.

He laughed. ''Cute. When that one shows up in the magazine I don't want to hear about it.''

She tossed him a cocky look as she headed into the building. ''You wouldn't dare.''

''You'd be amazed what I'd dare.'' Right now he was thinking hard about tossing her over his shoulder and dragging her behind one of these bushes and kissing her until she realized what a great thing they'd have. Even if it was for only a little while.

Her head whipped around, her eyes narrowed in warning. ''If that picture shows up in the magazine, Brady, you're fish food.''

He followed her down the corridors, laughing, enjoying the saucy kick of her hips as she strode in front of him. Even those Mother Teresa pants couldn't hide her sexy curves. Halfway down the corridor she stopped, pushed a door open and waved him in.

He stepped by her into the room. Four desks were

set up in a neat square in half of the room while a small lounge area with a coffee table, old, worn sofa and two overstuffed chairs occupied the other half. He turned back to her. "You were right, not illustrious. On the other hand, you have a great view." He pointed to the big picture window on the far wall.

"Yes, we do." She strode into the office, closing the door behind her.

He glanced around again. "Where is everyone?"

"Out in the field, I imagine. Ten of us actually share this office space and the computers, but we're in the field so often it's not unusual to find the place empty." She strode over to the biggest desk—the one that held the biggest computer—and set her purse on it.

Brady followed her. "So what do you do here?"

"I'll show you." She pushed the power button and sat, waiting for the machine to boot up.

He moved behind her so he could see the monitor, but being that close to her made him want to touch her. A temptation he quickly decided he didn't want to resist. He rested his hands on her shoulders. He held his breath. Would she shake them off? Tell him to behave?

She stilled, her shoulders tensing.

But she didn't tell him to get lost.

Yes. Quietly expelling his breath, he tried an easy massage, his fingers gently pushing into her shoulders.

There was a frame on her desk with a picture of

her and her family in it. But it wasn't the photo that held his attention. It was her reflection in the glass covering the picture. She looked tense, uncertain, as if she was trying to decide if she should indeed shake his hands loose.

He kept his touch absolutely therapeutic, his fingers moving gently, steadily over her shoulder muscles, making sure the massage was soothing, but not sensual—just one person giving another a relaxing massage, nothing more.

Slowly her shoulders relaxed and then he saw her eyes slowly drift shut in the framed piece of glass.

Okay, very good. He kept the massage steady for a bit, watching her reflection. As she relaxed, her features softened, the tense line of her jaw loosening, her lips parting slightly. She looked a little like he imagined she might after a night of lovemaking. Heat stole through him. He should stop, step back, but he didn't want to stop touching her and he wanted to know how much she'd allow. She said she was thinking about it. He wanted to know just how much.

He stroked his thumbs softly up her neck. Up and then back down. Lightly. Teasingly.

Her lips parted a little more at the sensuous touch and goose bumps raced over her skin.

He stroked her neck again.

She grimaced and her eyes popped open. "Okay, Brady, enough. You're not playing fair." She pulled away from him.

He dropped his hands and stepped back. "What

do you mean I'm not playing fair? I thought you looked a little tense. Thought a small neck rub would help.'' He injected as much innocence as he possibly could into his voice.

She shot him a dry look. "Yeah, right. Come on, this isn't playtime. I need you to concentrate on this now.'' She pointed to her monitor, shifting her own attention back to the screen.

"Does that mean it might be playtime later?'' he asked hopefully.

She chuckled softly. "I don't know, but pushing isn't going to help me decide. So be nice and pay attention here for now.''

He would rather be doing anything else, but she seemed determined to keep them on track. And the sooner they got this done the sooner they could get out of here. Then maybe he could do a little more coaxing. "Okay, I'm concentrating. What am I looking at? Besides a desktop full of icons.''

"Just watch. I'll explain after.'' She clicked on one of the icons.

Almost immediately an oceanscape appeared on the screen in two-dimensional form. Blue water, white sand and reefs filled with odd, colorful plant and animal life moved across the screen as if a diver was floating with a video camera in hand. Behind the reefs, a sea grass bed waved gently in the waves. Large splashes of red and orange moved across the screen as the imaginary diver floated by giant sponges. The delicate, translucent bodies of anemones swayed gently with the current. Hundreds of different kinds of fish teemed across the screen.

He snagged a nearby desk chair, dragged it over next to her and sat. "Very nice. But beyond an animated representation of the reefs, what am I looking at?"

"Hang on, you'll see."

As the image continued to move from right to left across the screen, the reefs gradually changed. The clear blue water took on a murky quality. The bed of sea grass disappeared. The coral beds diminished. Fewer and fewer anemones waved their delicate fingers across the screen. The big splashes of red and orange came by less and less often. The teeming schools of fish dwindled dramatically. Finally there was nothing on the screen but white sand, something that looked oddly like bleached broken bones lying on top of the sand and the occasional individual fish swimming by.

As the program came to an end, she clicked out of it and turned to him, waiting for his response.

Her look was so expectant, he was pretty sure she was looking for a specific response—but he didn't have a clue what it should be. He forged ahead blindly. "Okay, that looked like a pretty good representation of a dying reef."

She huffed at his answer. "How can you look at that and not be impressed? Not be alarmed?"

"I was impressed. The reef looked very...real. Very...lifelike."

She rolled her eyes. "That's because it is lifelike. In fact, it's an exceedingly accurate mockup of a stretch of reef right off the Florida Keys."

"Really? How accurate?" He leaned forward, pulled a small recorder out of his back pocket and set it on her desk. "You don't care if I record, do you? It's a lot more accurate than taking notes." And as long as the recorder was taking notes he could save his attention for her.

"Recording's fine." She waited for him to push the record button then continued. "As for how accurate, very. At least as accurate as we can humanly make it. For every piece of coral or bed of sea grass or sponge that you saw on the screen, there is a matching one in the ocean, located in the same place on the reef you saw it in the program."

She chuckled. "We took a little more artistic license with the fish, of course. We just can't get those guys to stay put. But we've put the fish on the screen as accurately as possible for where they were spotted on the reefs and the numbers they were spotted in."

Surprise skittered through him. "You *count* the fish?"

"You bet. As accurately as we can, anyway."

"That sounds like a lot of work. As a matter of fact, the whole deal sounds like a lot of work."

"It is. Way more work than we'd anticipated originally. We knew it was an ambitious project before we started, but we had no idea how quickly the parameters would broaden. Or how much work each of those parameters would require. And if the prototype is successful, those parameters will broaden a hundred fold.''

''What exactly is the point of all this work?''

''The point, of course, is to come up with a way to save the reefs. We're hoping this project will help us do that.''

He looked at the computer screen, then back to her. ''How does having a digital cousin of the reef do that?''

''Because what you're seeing isn't just a graphic reproduction of the reef. It's an interactive data program. Here's the idea behind the project. While we know some things that are causing problems in the reefs, we don't know others. For instance, we know that cutting down the mangrove forests was a disaster. It allowed sediment to flow into the ocean, smothering sea grass beds, muddying the water, burying some portions of the reefs, all of which led to an equal number of other problems—some that we know of, some that have undoubtedly slipped under our radar.''

He nodded. ''Okay, cutting down the mangroves was bad. Now what?''

''The stuff we don't know.'' Excitement sounded in her voice as she dived into the subject. ''For instance it was once thought that sewage from the Keys was infecting coral reefs offshore, causing diseases and killing the coral. But then one scientist wondered why reefs way off in the Caribbean, far enough away that the waste shouldn't be affecting them, were suffering from the same diseases. His theory now is that red, iron-rich dust from Africa brought over by transatlantic winds are carrying bacterial spores to the reefs. So he's studying correlations between dust and disease outbreaks.

"Which is what got me to thinking. What if there was a program we could load the health of the reefs into along with man-made and natural events and see if we could narrow down cause and effect. One of the biggest problems we have with the reefs is having so much information, it's impossible to process it all. Quite often by the time we've tried out several theories and finally stumbled along the right one, we've lost miles of reef. African sands case in point. So, I thought, wouldn't it be great if we had one program that could take the events information and the reef health information, put it together and come up with correlations long before one of us might think to look in that specific direction?" Pure passion sparkled in her eyes.

Now if he could just get her to send that passion in his direction. "That's a big order. Particularly if you're talking global events."

"Yeah, it is a big order. Fortunately, this prototype isn't that expansive. We're sticking to local events and, of course, our own reefs."

"And how is the program working out?"

"Good. We've narrowed a few things down, learned some important facts. But the project is young. Just six months old. And there is *so* much information to compile and feed into the program. The events, of course. Big engineering projects like dam building, new subdivisions, new highways, etcetera.'' She shook her head. ''I had no idea how many big projects were underway at any given moment here in Florida. Nor did I realize how many agencies I'd have to contact to get the information I need. Tracking them all down takes hours and hours.''

He could well imagine it did. And he could think of so many better ways for her to spend her time. At least while he was here. But he couldn't say that, either. He shifted his thoughts back to her research. ''The projects don't all affect the reefs, do they?''

''More of them than you'd think. It's that ripple effect. Drop a stone in the pond and the ripples just seem to go on forever. And then there's Mother Nature's fickle whims. Hurricanes, gully washers, tidal waves, that kind of thing. Obviously, something as big and occasional as a hurricane is easy to record, but there are a million smaller events that aren't as easy to track down. I never realized there were so many tropical storms just off our coast, storms we never feel here on land, but which very well could affect the water offshore. Not to mention the number of small local gully washers and microbursts that go on here on land. It's an amazing amount of data. And that's only on the events side of the equation.''

"I imagine you have just as much data to collect on the reef side."

"Absolutely. Water samples, soil samples, algae samples, species samples—and there are thousands and thousands of species down there. Plus every occurrence of disease is cataloged. And the disease is overwhelming, more and more every day. New diseases are showing up constantly, which requires even more collection and research. It's a daunting task."

"It sounds daunting. So daunting in fact, that I think you need an evening of rest and relaxation tonight." He mentally crossed his fingers. "How about a little dinner and dancing when we finish here?"

Irritation flashed across her face. "Dinner and dancing? *Brady,* I need you to focus here. We're discussing the reefs, remember?"

"Of course, I remember. Cutting down mangrove forests is bad, and African dust may or may not be causing disease in the coral. I'm not ignoring the reefs. I'm just taking a little break and asking a pretty lady out."

She crossed her arms over her chest and shot him an admonishing look.

"Come on, Laura," he coaxed, running his finger down her arm, reminding her how good it had felt on her neck. Encouraging her to think about how good it might feel on other parts of her body. "It's only a little dinner, a little dancing, no big deal."

She shot him a black scowl and slapped his hand. "Stop it. This is a business office. And it *is* a big deal. This article is important to me. I need you concentrating on it right now. As for tonight, we have dinner with my folks, remember?''

''Oh, damn. I forgot. Couldn't we postpone it, have dinner with them tomorrow night?''

''Trust me, that would not be a wise decision. We miss dinner, and my father and brothers would be waiting on my porch when we came back from dinner and dancing. So we are going to my folks tonight—without fail. And until then, I expect you to pay attention. Got it?''

A forlorn sigh echoed through his head. An afternoon of reefs and an evening of being vetted by a no-doubt overprotective set of parents. Definitely not the scenario he'd hoped for. Definitely not the scenario his libido clamored for. But he managed to nod his head. ''Got it.''

Five

Laura cast a covert glance at Brady as she drove to her parents' estate. Dressed in a pair of butter-soft jeans and a dark green shirt that brought out the green in his eyes, he made her mouth water and every nerve in her body hum with need. He was so gorgeous.

And charming.

And sexy.

And just so damned fun to be around.

Even when he was driving her crazy. And he'd driven her megacrazy at work today. Getting him to focus on work instead of her had been impossible. By the time they'd left the office she'd wanted to strangle him. This article was so important to her, not only on a professional level, but on a personal one as well. This article was the best chance she was going to have at making her family understand how important her job was. Making them understand that she *wasn't* wasting her life.

She mentally shook her head. Still trying to gain parental acceptance at thirty. Pitiful. But there it was. She was tired of feeling like an outsider when she was with her family. Tired of feeling like the odd duck out. She wanted them to accept her for who she was. Love her for who she was. She didn't want to feel that their love and acceptance hinged upon her desire to join the family business.

But if she didn't find a way to get Brady to focus on his reason for being here, all would be lost. Which meant *she* needed to concentrate on the reason he was here and not the sexy fit of his jeans. Or the tantalizing proposition he'd tossed out last night.

"So, is this going to be a you-better-not-write-anything-mean-about-our-daughter dinner?" Brady asked from the passenger seat.

She pushed those sexy, distracting thoughts away and shook her head. "No. Well, I don't know, there might be some of that. We've certainly had trouble with nosy reporters lately. But I think my parents' main concern is that you're staying with me. My guess is they just want to make sure you aren't a serial killer or some other nefarious character."

His lips twisted in a crooked smile. "Think I should have worn my I'm-a-respectful-honest-and-trustworthy-guy T-shirt?"

She laughed, shaking her head. "I think you're fine just the way you are." More than fine. Another thought she resolutely pushed away as she turned into the driveway that led to her parents' estate and stopped in front of the big iron gates that protected the property. She zipped her window down, grabbed the card key from her purse, swiped it through the slot and drove in when the gates opened.

"Wow. Pretty fancy."

She tossed him a teasing grin. "Keeps the nosy reporters out."

He laughed. "I'll bet."

She drove up the curving driveway until she hit the circular path that wound in front of the sprawling two-story house. "This is it." She parked the car and climbed out.

He followed and they climbed the wide stone staircase to the front door together. Pulling the door open, she waved him in. "Welcome to my parents' home." She followed him into the spacious foyer.

He looked around at the marble floors, giant chandeliers, winding staircase and exotic flower arrangements. "Very nice."

She shrugged. "Outrageous decadence, but my parents are into that kind of thing." The sound of voices wafted to them from straight ahead. "Come on, sounds like everyone's in the ocean room."

She led him through big double doors. While she thought her parents' home was the epitome of conspicuous consumption, she loved this room where floor-to-ceiling windows made up the entire front wall, offering a breathtaking view of the ocean and letting the sun stream in, in glorious golden rays. She looked over to catch Brady's reaction.

He was staring out at the ocean with pure appreciation.

"Beautiful, isn't it?"

He nodded. "Breathtaking."

"There you are, dear." Her mother rose from the couch and headed her way, her arms open.

Laura stepped into the embrace for a quick hug. "Hi, Mom. You all surviving the heat?"

"Best we can. Luckily, the house is nice and cool."

Laura bit back her retort on the sins of air-conditioning, particularly on the grand scale it took to cool this monstrosity. It was an argument that only made everyone unhappy. So she swallowed her words and managed a smile. "Yep, that's nice on days like this." She stepped back and waved a hand toward Brady. "Mom, I'd like you to meet Austin Brady, the reporter from *Land, Sea & Sky Magazine*. Mr. Brady, my mom, Lynn Evans."

He extended his hand. "Mrs. Evans, it's a pleasure to meet you."

Surprise crossed her mother's face as she extended her hand. "Brady?"

"Brady," Laura confirmed. "*Land, Sea & Sky* sent a different reporter than they'd originally planned."

Her mother's smile never wavered. "Well, it's nice to meet you, Mr. Brady. And please, call me Lynn. Everyone does."

Brady gave his head a single nod. "Only if you call me Austin."

Laura turned to the only other person in the room. "And this is my sister-in-law, Emma."

Emma, who'd already joined the group, extended her hand to the reporter.

He enclosed it in his. "Nice to meet you, Emma."

Laura smiled. "Emma married my brother, Seth, about six weeks ago. Which you might have already heard since it, too, was in all the papers. And they are currently expecting my first niece or nephew." She didn't even try to keep the excitement from her voice. She couldn't wait for the little munchkin to make its entrance into the world.

Brady smiled and gave Emma's hand another shake. "Congratulations."

Emma laughed. "Thank you. Seth and I are almost as excited as Laura."

"And speaking of Seth," Laura said. "Where is he? And Dad and Holt?"

"You know those three," her mother commented. "They wandered off to talk a little business. I'm sure they'll join us soon. Until then, why don't you two have a seat with Emma and I'll have Jeanne bring drinks. What would you like, Austin?"

Laura rolled her eyes. "Oh no, I'm not going to sit around and wait for those three to show up. If someone doesn't drag them back, we won't see them until the night's over. I'll go dig them up."

Brady turned to her. "Do you want me to go with you?"

Absolutely not. The men were no doubt locked away in her dad's study talking boats. If Brady went with her, *he'd* probably end up talking boats—every little boy's, teenage boy's and grown man's favorite hobby from what she'd observed in life. And if that happened she'd never get his attention back to the reefs. The whole article would turn into a boat parade. How they used this type of boat to get to the reefs, and how that type of boat was better for fishing while this type of boat was better for diving. And if you were looking for pure comfort and luxury on the water, an Evans yacht was surely your best pick. She *wasn't* going to let that happen.

She shook her head. "And leave Emma alone while Mom goes to order everyone's drinks? Besides, if you come, I can't lecture them about their bad manners. Have a seat and I'll be right back." She zipped off before he could argue with her.

As she approached her dad's study, the men's voices drifted down the hall. She shook her head. Her father had spent his entire life building boats and running Evans Yachts. On the day Russ Evans had stepped down three years ago as CEO, her older brother, Seth, had assumed the role. Holt, her younger brother, had spent his life testing and racing the sleek, quick, vessels. And *still* they never got enough of their toys.

As she approached the open study door, her father's voice became clear. "Have you heard from Marcus on the charter clients Drew was flying around a few weeks back?"

"As a matter of fact I have," Seth answered. "And the news isn't good. Drew was right. Those men definitely weren't tourists. And they were definitely up to no good.''

Laura jerked to attention at her brother's words. *And they were definitely up to no good.* That sounded ominous. Had she happened upon a conversation that might tell her what was really going on in her family? She hoped so. She didn't like being kept in the dark. She stepped into the study. "What clients of Drew's? And what kind of no-good were they up to?''

All three men started at the sound of her voice, their gazes whipping in her direction.

Her father recovered himself first, smoothing the surprised look from his face and pasting a broad smile in its place. "Laura, you're early. Did you bring your reporter?''

"I'm not early, Dad. As usual when you gentlemen talk boats, you lost track of time. It's six o'clock. Six-ten, actually. And yes, I've brought the reporter. Now, answer my question. What's up with Drew's clients?''

Her father waved away her question. "Nothing important. We were just talking, idle chatter. And completely off the subject we were supposed to be discussing. So why—''

"Oh, no. You're not going to shut me out that easily. Something is going on in this family and I want to know what it is.'' Frustration curled in her belly. "I'm worried.''

"Well, quit worrying," her father reassured. "Nothing's going on."

She dug her heels in, determined not to let them brush her aside this time. "Really? Is that why Seth has hired extra security at Evans Yachts?"

Seth leveled his I'm-trying-to-be-a-patient-big-brother look on her. "I hired extra security to protect the secrecy of the *Unicorn.* I already explained that to you."

"Yes, you told me. But I don't believe the new racing yacht you're building for Holt is the cause of everything that's going on."

"The fact that you don't want to believe me doesn't make it untrue. You know as well as anyone in this family how competitive the yacht-racing industry is. This isn't the first time someone has tried to steal the plans for a new boat. Or break into the plant and take pictures of a new craft."

"No, it isn't. But this *is* the first time Evans Yachts has been plagued by so many odd occurrences, such as your boat blowing up, a continual change of personal assistants for you, and last, but certainly not least, someone trying to kidnap your fiancée."

A chill shot through her as she thought of the moment on Seth and Emma's original wedding day when two thugs had grabbed Emma, shoved her on one of their Sea-doos and tried to make off with her. Thank God Seth had been able to chase them down in another boat and rescue Emma.

Laura pulled her mind from the scary thought and centered it on the case at hand. "And this *is* the first time you've hired so much extra security."

Seth sighed. "The explosion on *Strictly Business* was an accident. I told you that. As for Emma's kidnapping, obviously whoever is after the specs on Holt's boat is more serious than other competitors we've run into in the past. Which is why I've hired extra security. End of story."

She shook her head. "I don't believe it. I've been through that before. This *feels* different. There's something more going on here than someone trying to steal the specs to Holt's boat. And for some reason you think I should be kept in the dark about it."

"Laura, dear, what possible reason would we have to keep you in the dark about anything?" Her father broke in with his calm voice of reason.

Laura turned on him, tossing her hands in exasperation. "God knows. What was your point of keeping me in the dark about Marcus and his other newly found brothers and sisters?"

They all exchanged a guilty look.

"That was different," her father said.

"How do you figure? Last time I looked, Marcus was my cousin, too."

"Come on, Laura," Holt broke in. "*We* didn't even know what was going on until it was practically over."

Laura narrowed her eyes on her younger brother. She was closer to Holt than anyone else in the family. But even *he* had kept the secret about Marcus and his newfound brothers and sisters. A defection that had stung. "Maybe not. But the truth is, even after it was over you weren't going to tell me."

"No, I wasn't," her father said without a hint of apology. "The Coalition wasn't playing games, Laura. They were a rogue band of scientists that had been involved in the genetic engineering of six children. Five of which they'd hoped to turn into their very own world-toppling, criminal organization. One of which was your cousin Marcus. What father in his right mind would want to embroil his daughter in that mess?"

"The point is I had a right to decide for myself if I wanted to be embroiled or not."

"Laura, what if you had known?" Holt asked. "What would you have done? We're talking Marcus here. You know, superman? Superfast, superstrong, practically superhuman. Of course, we now know he didn't come by any of that naturally. The scientists helped make him that way. But the bottom line is what do you think you could have done that Marcus couldn't have?"

Frustration boiled through her. "Maybe all I could have done was worry. But I had a right to worry. This is my family, too, despite the fact you all seem to want to keep me out of it."

"No one's trying to keep you out of it," her father said in his authoritative tone. "In fact, we've been trying to get you to join the family business for years.''

She sighed at the old argument, pain slicing through her. ''And what? I can't be a member of the family until I join the business?''

''That's not what I said.''

''Yeah, Dad, it is.'' She paced away, plowing her fingers through her hair. When was her family going to accept her for who and what she was? She pushed that futile thought aside, refocused on her original question and turned back to the three men clustered around her father's desk. ''So are you going to tell me what's going on with Drew's clients or not?''

Her father splayed his hands. ''Nothing to tell.''

She looked at her father and Seth, so alike with their light brown hair, brown eyes and workaholic, hard-nosed characters. Both of their faces were set. They weren't going to budge one bit on their story. She glanced to Holt, the family's golden boy with his blond hair and blue eyes and charming, carefree attitude. His mouth was pressed into a thin, hard line—dead giveaway that he wasn't happy about the family line but he was going to hold to it.

She shook her head. ''Fine. Keep whatever's going on to yourselves. But you all have to come join the party now. This little shindig was your idea, Dad. I expect you to be there for it.''

They obviously weren't happy about the abrupt end to their meeting, but they knew she wouldn't leave the room without them. They reluctantly pushed up from their seats, grabbed their drinks and followed her from the room.

She looked back over her shoulder, giving her father a pointed look. "And I'd appreciate it if you all refrained from talking business during the party. I was nice enough to go along with your checking out the reporter so you and Mom wouldn't have to worry about me. So I don't think it's too much to ask for it to be a fun, relaxed evening." If she could keep boats from being mentioned at all tonight, so much the better.

She led the way back to the party, her father and brothers following close behind. Entering the ocean room, she found her mom and Emma sitting on one sofa and Brady sitting across from them on the opposing one.

The conversation ceased the moment they strode in, her mother looking over her shoulder. "Oh good, Laura found you all. Come meet Mr. Brady. Well, actually he prefers to be called Austin. He was just telling us about his trip here. Apparently, it went quite smoothly." Her mother stood, waiting for them to join them all at the sofas.

Brady stood the moment her mother did.

Laura strode up to him, her dad and brothers at her heels. "I'd like you to meet my father and brothers. Russ Evans, Seth and Holt."

Her father's brow lifted as he shook Brady's hand. "Austin Brady?"

Brady smiled good-naturedly. "Not who you were expecting, is it?"

"Sorry. Laura told us the magazine was sending Dean Michaels." Her father's tone was casual enough, but Laura caught the slight narrowing of his eyes. Felt his sudden interest, or perhaps suspicion, in the change of plan.

She sighed inwardly, sensing a barrage of questions about to come the reporter's way.

But Brady answered the note of inquiry in her father's statement with an easy nod. "And so they were. But when the new volcano erupted, *Land, Sea & Sky Magazine,* like everyone else, sent their most qualified reporters to the location. Which in their case was the reporter they'd assigned to Laura's profile."

Her father took her mother's elbow, escorting her back to her seat. "So how did you fall heir to the assignment?"

"I'm a personal friend of Caleb Jacobs, the editor who's behind the profile on Laura. So when he needed a fill-in reporter, he called me."

Her father's expression sharpened as he sat down beside her mother. "You don't work for *Land, Sea & Sky*?"

Brady shook his head, taking Laura's elbow much as her father had done and leading her to the spot next to where he'd been sitting.

She should probably object, but at the moment a little support felt good. She sat beside him, taking far more comfort from his presence and warmth than she should have.

"I'm freelance, actually," Brady said, handing her the drink he or her mother had obviously ordered for her, and then picking up his own. "But since I'd just finished up my last assignment and hadn't decided on anything new, I was happy to help him out."

She took the glass, noticing the pink blush to the wine and the lemon twist. A kir. Brady had remembered what she'd had the other night and ordered the same for her tonight. Her parents always served her Chardonnay, no questions asked. Smiling, she downed a fortifying swallow.

"Lucky for both of you that you were free," her father said, still on his fishing expedition. "Have you known Caleb long?"

"We met in college. Had a few journalism classes together. And kept in touch after graduation."

Poor Caleb. Her dad would no doubt call him first thing in the morning to check out his friend's credentials.

Leaning back against the sofa, her father crossed his ankle over his knee. "You mentioned you'd just finished up a previous assignment. Anything interesting?"

The question sounded casual enough, but Laura wasn't fooled. She could sense her father's alertness. There wasn't anything casual about his question.

Luckily, Brady didn't seem to notice. He nodded.

"It was interesting. The piece is called 'Life in a Dictatorship.' *Time* will be publishing it in October."

"That does sound interesting. Was this book research or actual, you-were-there stuff?"

Laura took another sip of her kir, studying her father. He was watching Austin Brady like a hawk, observing, accessing.

Brady took a sip of his drink before answering. "A little bit of both. I did a ton of research and then spent six months both openly and in disguise in countries like North Korea, Cuba, Rebelia."

Her father's eyes narrowed imperceptibly. "Rebelia?"

Brady nodded. "Are you familiar with it?"

Her father tipped a shoulder. "A little. It's a small Eastern European country, right? Taken over a few years ago by a rogue military leader, wasn't it?"

Laura raised a brow at her father's answer. He knew more than a little about Rebelia and its current dictator. For pity's sake, Rebelia had been the country trying to assassinate Samantha, the woman Marcus had married last year.

Brady nodded. "Bruno DeBruzkya. Rebelia was a quiet little country before he took over. But his murder of the royal family made the headlines. And he was in the news linked with the genetic engineering stories not too long ago. Then there was his takeover of Holzberg, the small seacoast country between him and the sea. That made the news more recently."

"Of course, I'm remembering the articles now. And you were in Rebelia?"

"Six weeks. It's a country with a lot of potential."

Her father's eyes narrowed a hair more at that comment. "An interesting observation for a war-torn country. Did you see DeBruzkya's headquarters? I heard it was an old castle in the mountains somewhere."

He'd heard it was an old castle in the mountains somewhere? Her dad *knew* DeBruzkya's headquarters were in Veisweimar castle. And he knew exactly where in the northern mountain region that castle stood. Why was he pretending he didn't know anything?

She cast a quick glance at Seth and Holt. They, too, were watching Brady with more attention than the conversation called for. Even Emma seemed more interested than normal. What was going on? Why had Brady's trip to Rebelia created so much interest? Negative interest, if she was reading her father and brothers right. Well, whatever was going on, she was going to put a stop to it before Brady realized he was in the middle of an inquisition instead of a conversation.

"So, Emma," she broke in. "How's the nursery going?"

Emma snapped her attention to Laura, a little surprised at the question. "The nursery?"

Laura laughed. "Yeah, you know, a room for the baby. Cribs, rocking chairs, mobiles, that kind of thing. Last time I talked to you, choosing the right motif was a priority in your life. How's it going?''

Emma hesitated, looking at her father-in-law, no doubt waiting to see if he would push the conversation back to Rebelia.

''Why are you looking at him? He's not helping with the nursery, is he?'' Laura asked, injecting a teasing note in her voice. She wanted to keep everything on an easy note, but she was determined to leave the inquisition behind.

''God, no,'' her father said. ''I leave the decorating to the members in this family who can tell blue from green.''

Everyone laughed, including Brady.

Good. Her father was going to let the subject go.

''So, Emma,'' Laura said, ''what motif did you pick?''

''We…'' She looked away, a pink flush coloring her cheeks. ''We decided on sailboats,'' she finished in a rush.

Laura groaned. ''Oh man, you're going to start indoctrinating the kid from the moment he's born.''

''Now, Laura,'' her mother said. ''Emma showed me a sample of the wallpaper she ordered. It's very pretty.''

Laura rolled her eyes. ''I'm sure it is, Mom.''

''And if we're lucky,'' Emma said, her excitement about preparing for her first child taking over, ''it will arrive next week and then we can pick the paint and carpet and get started on remodeling. I'm hoping to have it done for the regatta so I can show it off to everyone.''

"The regatta?'' Brady asked.

Oh God, Laura didn't want the conversation to go there.

But before she could redirect the conversation, her mother said, "It's a big bash. Friends, family, business associates come from all over the world. We have games and huge buffets during the day. Fancy dinners and dancing at night. But the big attraction is the boat races. We have speedboat races, catamaran races, even big, luxury yacht races. Everyone who can sails in so they can participate. It's great fun.''

"It sounds like fun.'' Excitement flared in Brady's eyes.

Excitement she'd tried to generate all day for her reefs. To no avail. But now, just mention the word *boat*...

"It is fun,'' her father said. "And this year will be even more exciting than usual because Holt will be debuting the new boat Seth just built for him.''

Brady looked to her younger brother. "Really? Its first race?''

Holt nodded. "It's going to be one hell of a race this year. The *Unicorn*'s fast. Very fast.'' Pure anticipation brightened his expression.

"Are you into boats, Austin?'' her father asked.

Austin cocked a brow in amusement. "You know a man who isn't?''

Her father smiled. "Haven't met him yet. But I'm sure he's out there. If you'd like I'll arrange a tour of the plant while you're here. You can see firsthand how we build the boats."

"I'd love it."

Laura slumped back against the sofa, her fingers strangling the thin stem of her wineglass. They were off and running now. There would be no stopping them. They were going to talk boats until dinner was over and she dragged Brady away. And he was going to enjoy it a hundred times more than anything she'd told him all day. Damn, damn, *damn*.

She took a giant sip of wine, frustration pounding through her. First she'd been reminded that, while the same blood ran in her veins, she wasn't really a part of this family. And now they were going to steal her reporter away and woo him with boats and tours until he probably wouldn't even remember he'd come down here to do a story on her reefs. Could this night possibly get any worse?

Just then Jeanne strode in from the kitchens.

Her mother turned to her. "Is dinner ready, dear?"

Jeanne gave her head a single nod. "Yes, ma'am."

Her mother looked to Austin with her beaming hostess's smile. "I had the cook prepare a special dinner for you. Fresh lobster. Pulled from the ocean just this morning."

Six

Russell Evans stood next to his wife as they watched their daughter and Austin Brady head to her car. Russ's gaze was locked on the reporter's back, the word *freelance* echoing uncomfortably in his head. When they were both in the car and Laura had turned the engine over, Russ and his wife gave them a final wave.

As soon as they started down the driveway, Lynn turned to him. "I take it you four had words in the study. Laura was tense and upset when you all came back to the ocean room. And she didn't relax much the rest of the evening, either."

He shrugged. "She thinks we're hiding something from her. Keeping her out of the loop."

"We are."

"To keep her safe."

"Yes, but she doesn't know that. And I'm not sure she'd care if she did. I know when I discovered you'd all kept what was going on from me I didn't like it one bit."

And if the line furrowing her brow meant anything, she hadn't completely forgiven him for keeping those secrets, either. He ran a hand down her shoulder. "I apologized for that. And you understood why I didn't tell you. You understood I wanted to keep you from worrying. That I thought you'd be safer if you didn't know."

"I understood because I love you and know how wide your protective streak is. But it wasn't fair and I don't think keeping what's going on from Laura is fair, either."

"But you're not going to interfere?"

Her lips pressed into a thin line, but she shook her head. "Not for now. But I want you to think about this. I know you love your daughter and I know you believe she's safer not knowing about what's going on. But..."

"But what?"

She tipped her head to the side. "Are you sure you're not keeping her out of the loop to force her hand? Making her feel she doesn't quite belong so she'll give in and join the business?"

"Do you think I'm that petty?"

She smiled. "I don't think there's a petty bone in your body. But I do think you're a determined man. And you've always wanted all of the children to be part of Evans Yachts."

"I thought you did, too."

"I do. But Laura's thirty. I think at some point we're going to have to at least entertain the idea that she's chosen her career. And it isn't boats."

A sense of loss squeezed his chest. He'd worked hard all his life to build Evans Yachts into the powerhouse it was today. He wanted his children to enjoy the fruits of that labor. All of them. "I'm not giving up on her yet."

Lynn smiled. "Okay, I won't argue with you. For now. Are you coming to bed, or do you boys have more business to discuss?"

He pushed a stray strand of hair behind her ear, drinking in her beauty. They'd both left their youth far behind, but to him she just got more beautiful every day. "Sorry. We have a bit more business to hash out, but if you wait up for me, I'll make it worth your time."

She smiled up at him with a saucy grin. "I'll be waiting. Don't dillydally." She rose up on her toes, gave him a quick, deep kiss and sashayed off, her hips swaying seductively.

Dillydally? Absolutely not. He turned on his heel and strode to his study. Holt and Seth were waiting for him when he arrived. Good. They could get this business taken care of and then he could get on to more interesting matters.

"Let's get the business of Drew's 'tourists' out of the way and then we can tackle Laura's reporter. What did Marcus's buddies have to say about Drew's tourists?" Russ strode to his desk and sat, thinking about his nephew Marcus. When his brother and sister-in-law had trouble conceiving a second child after having their first son, Drew, they'd adopted Marcus. They'd had no idea at the time that the boy had been part of a genetics engineering project. They'd always thought his physical abilities a fluke of nature. But whatever the origin of those abilities, they'd made the man the perfect Navy SEAL. And the intelligence contacts Marcus had made during that time, and kept in touch with since, had come in damned handy lately.

"As we all suspected, thanks to Marcus's warning to keep our eyes open, the supposed tourists were Rebelian spies," Seth said.

Russ swore softly. "Well, now we know De-Bruzkya's after our secret. The trick will be to make sure he doesn't get it."

"Why hasn't someone shot that little bastard?" Holt asked, propping his ankle on his knee and rocking back in his chair.

Russ grimaced. "Good question. But until someone does, we need to be on our toes."

Seth nodded. "I've already beefed up security at the factory. And with cyber-theft what it is these days, I've asked Gideon to make sure our firewalls are strong. He's creating new programs now. And he suggested it might not be a bad idea to encrypt anything DeBruzkya might be interested in."

"Sounds like a damned good idea," Russ said, thinking of Gideon Faulkner, one of Marcus's newfound brothers. One of the genetically engineered children. Seth had hired him at Evans Yachts when he'd learned that the gift the scientists had endowed upon Gideon was an uncanny ability to imagine and invent new technologies. An ability that had come in

JUDITH LYONS   91

handy with the project currently underway at Evans
Yachts. The project DeBruzkya wanted to get his
hands on. And now they would use Gideon's keen
knack with computers to help keep the project from
falling into the wrong hands.

"I thought it was a good idea, too," Seth said,
"which is why when he suggested bringing his sister,
Gretchen, in to do the encryption work, I told him to
go ahead and invite her in."

"Gretchen is the cryptographer, right?"

Seth nodded. "World renowned."

"Well, genetic engineering obviously has its ad-
vantages," Russ observed. "And if an impermeable
intelligence system can be created, I imagine those
two can do it. Is she on her way?"

"She arrives tomorrow."

"Good. I'll increase security during the regatta as
well."

"That'll be DeBruzkya's best chance of getting
what he wants," Holt said. "The house isn't as easy
to protect as the offices, and with all the people at
the regatta, it will be the one time when a stray face
won't stand out."

Russ nodded. "Which is why we're having the big
meeting with the navy then. Hopefully, no one will
notice the naval officers, either. But you're right, it
will be our most vulnerable time. I'll have to make
sure we have enough protection to cover our asses.
Which takes care of that bit of business. Now, have

we heard back on the soda can Drew sent to Marcus for fingerprint analysis?''

''That one the spies drank from when Drew was showing them around?'' Seth asked.

Russ nodded.

Seth grimaced. ''Marcus wasn't able to lift any usable prints. Dead end.''

''Damn. Okay, let's move on. Anyone else uncomfortable that we've had a change of reporters?''

''And the fact that he's recently spent time in Rebelia? Absolutely,'' Seth said.

Holt took a sip of the drink he'd carried back with him. ''We might be a little paranoid here. After all, there is a new volcano forming in the Pacific. It wouldn't be unreasonable to think *Land, Sea & Sky* had a last-minute change of plan. And Brady's reason for being in Rebelia sounded equally legitimate.''

''Yes, but Brady's a blip on the radar. And with everything that's going on, I think the smartest course is to keep all the blips identified right now. Particularly since the man is staying with your sister.''

Holt's expression turned grim. ''You're right.''

Seth nodded. ''I'll call Marcus first thing tomorrow morning. Let him check with his buddies in intelligence again, make sure the guy's clean.''

Russ gave his head a nod of agreement. ''Good. And in the future, we're going to have to be more careful about talking about this problem when Laura might be lurking around.''

Holt grimaced. ''If we tell her what's going on we won't have to be careful.''

Russ shook his head. ''I don't want her to know. As long as she's not in the loop, she's not a target. I want to keep it that way.''

Holt's lips pressed into a hard line. ''I disagree. I think as long as her last name is Evans, she could be a target. And keeping her in the dark about something this big, this dangerous, isn't nice, or smart. She should be keeping her eyes open for trouble just like the rest of us. And when she does find out what we're keeping from her, there's going to be hell to pay.''

''No one has a reason to go after her if she can't tell them anything. Which right now she can't. I don't want to change that.'' Russ looked to Seth.

Seth nodded. ''I agree. She's safer not knowing.''

Holt rolled his eyes at his older brother. ''Of course you agree. You're as much of a control freak as Dad is.''

Russ looked back to Holt. ''You could trust the fact that your old man has a little more experience in the world than you do. Give me the benefit of the doubt that I'm making the best decision here.''

His youngest son stared at him, his blue eyes sharp and unwavering.

Russ didn't know whether to smile or growl in frustration. Holt was a maverick. A self-thinker. He didn't like being told what to do. He never had. He liked to run wild with the wind, which was probably the quality that made him such an outstanding racer. But sometimes his wild ways made life damned difficult.

Finally Holt gave an assenting nod. "Fine. For now. I'll go along with you, but more because I don't want to risk her reporter catching wind of anything than because I want to give you that benefit of the doubt. The last thing we need right now is a leak to the press. But I reserve the right to change my mind at any point. And when this decision comes back to bite you in the ass, don't forget I told you so."

Russ nodded, smiling wryly. "I appreciate your support. Even if it's begrudgingly given." After all, his children were long past the point where he could tell them what to do. And they all knew it. "That's it, then. I'll see you all tomorrow morning." He pushed up from his desk and strode from the office. He had a lady waiting for him.

Laura walked through her front door, propped the wooden portal open, stalked through the house and opened the back door, too. It had to be a million degrees in here. Perfect. Just one more irritant to add to this day.

Frustration washing over her, she stormed into the kitchen, jerked the fridge open and pulled out the peanut butter, strawberry jam and a loaf of bread.

She set them on the counter with a thump just as Brady finally wandered into the house from the car.

He looked over at her, his expression hesitant. Finally he said, "That was a pretty quiet ride home."

"Ya think?" She grabbed a butter knife from the drawer and dug out a glob of peanut butter. She couldn't remember when an evening had gone so badly.

He tipped his head, studying her. "Are you mad at me?"

She slathered the peanut butter on a slice of bread and pointed the butter knife at him. "You ate that poor lobster."

He splayed his hands in supplication. "What was I supposed to do? Insult your mother by not eating it?"

"Yes," she snapped, adding jelly to the peanut butter and slapping another piece of bread on top.

He made a face, hanging his hands on his hips. "I thought you said you don't hold others to your beliefs."

She scowled at him as she strode over to the sofa and dropped into its leather folds. "I lied." She took a giant bite of the sandwich, trying to chase away her hunger and frustration.

He strode over to the sofa and dropped down on the other end of it. "Come on, you're not really mad at me for eating that lobster, are you?"

She shot him another scowl. "Brady, you didn't

just eat the poor thing. You enjoyed every last bite. *Relished* every bite.''

Guilt crossed his face. "It *was* good.''

She snorted at his answer and downed another bite of PB&J.

"Come on, Laura, you can't totally blame me. Don't your parents know you don't eat your friends?''

She sighed, the frustration of the situation washing through her. "Yes, they do. But they don't get it. They never have. When I was thirteen, fourteen, they thought it was cute, and they humored me for a while. But by the time I was sixteen, they just thought it was ridiculous. They couldn't understand why I hadn't outgrown what they thought was a childish sentiment. At that point it turned into a big family battle, Mom trying to feed me seafood, me refusing and everyone at the table ending up mad and upset. So I quit complaining. I let her put it in front of me and I just didn't eat it.''

"Which is what you're still doing today.''

"Yep, pretty much.'' She took another bite. Why couldn't her family just let her be who she was? And why did she let them push her around?

"You're an adult now. Why don't you make your case again?''

"Because they wouldn't understand it any more today than they did then. And it would cause the same bad feelings.''

"And you don't want them to feel bad.''

"I hate it when they're upset. I want them to be happy."

He shook his head, smiling. "You're a softy, Laura Evans."

"No, I'm not. I'm a wimp."

She sighed. "No, you're not. If you were a wimp you'd be keeping your mouth shut because it was easier for you. You're keeping your mouth shut because you don't want to make them unhappy, even though it makes you crazy. That's a softy."

She rolled her eyes. "Yeah, right."

He cocked his head, studying her. "So are you mad at me—or your family?"

"Both." She plowed a hand through her hair. "And I'm not just mad. I'm worried."

"Worried? About your family?"

She nodded.

"Why?"

Because they're lying to me about something. Something bad.

She could feel it clear down to her bones. But now that she'd opened her big fat mouth, she wasn't sure she should have said anything to Brady. The man was a journalist. And while he wasn't an investigative reporter, she thought journalists in general had an inquisitive nature. If she told him she was worried about some threat to her family, might he start poking his nose into her family's business?

If he did, she might find out what was going on, which would be nice. But he could also stumble on the information that her cousin Marcus was one of the people the press had dubbed the Proteans, the children created by the scientists involved in Code Proteus, the secret genetic engineering program from the sixties. If Brady came up with that information, would he be able to resist the temptation to go public with it?

The press had done its best to uncover the exact details of Code Proteus and to identify the children who'd been the results of the experiments. Luckily, they'd been unsuccessful to date. She'd hate to change that now. While some of the press had been responsible in their reporting, many of them had not been, sensationalizing the story and painting the Proteans as sinister monsters, which had put many citizens into a panicked frenzy.

If the public found out who the Proteans were, their lives would be hell. And since the Proteans were anything but sinister monsters, despite the Coalition's attempts to make them so, the last thing she wanted was for their identities to be discovered.

She waved away his question. "Never mind. I'm just tired and stressed-out. My dad has always wanted me to quit working at the institute and join the family business. These past two years, as he sees me getting older, he's really started putting on the pressure. It's just…exhausting sometimes."

"Did you and your dad have a fight about that before you came out to join us?"

She grimaced. "How'd you guess?" It wasn't the whole truth, but it was part of it.

"I could think of a few ways to make you forget all about tonight. Get you to relax." His voice was low, suggestive, and he had that charming, sexy smile on his lips.

She laughed, shaking her head. "You're good, Brady. Very good. But I'm not that easy. And besides, I'm mad at you, too. Remember?"

He sighed, a sad, fatalistic sound. "For eating the lobster."

She nodded. "And for being so damned excited over the boat talk while you did it."

The same sparkle of excitement he'd had in his eye all night came back. "It was fascinating, listening to the way your grandfather and father built Evans Yachts. I can't wait to see the boatyard."

She looked at him in disgust. "Do you have any idea how hard I tried to generate that enthusiasm in you today at the lab?"

"Hey, I paid attention at the lab."

"Paid attention, yes. *Barely*. When you weren't trying to seduce me."

He smiled unabashedly. "Well, a man has to keep his priorities straight."

She shot him a sideways glance. "Your priority is supposed to be the article."

He pointed an admonishing finger at her. "Stop worrying about your article. It's going to be fine. But you can't honestly think that given a choice between a bunch of slow-growing reefs and a beautiful woman, the reefs are going to come out on top. Nor are they going to come out on top when you compare them with boats. Fish and coral simply aren't as exciting as skimming along the waves at an exhilarating pace.''

That was it! She pinned him with a hard stare. ''You don't know what you're talking about. You think because you've gone snorkeling a few times you know what the ocean is all about?'' She shook her head. ''You don't have a clue. But you're about to.''

She pushed up from the sofa, stalked over to the bookcase, jerked out the introductory-to-diving book and tossed it on the coffee table. ''Study up, buddy. You're going scuba diving. And when you come back up from your first dive we'll see what's more exciting—skimming along the water or swimming with the fishes.''

Seven

Austin stood on the deck of the yacht as they skimmed along the top of the water, his camera hanging comfortably around his neck. He and Laura had spent the past two days at the Long Key lab while Laura fed him more facts on the reefs. Boring. Facts and figures, experimentation and theories just weren't his thing. He'd had a lot more fun in the evenings when Laura had taken him to her neighbor's pool to teach him how to scuba.

She'd had to take off her Mother Teresa suits then and put on one of her bathing suits, giving him an opportunity to enjoy all her golden skin and luscious curves. And she was more relaxed at night when she wasn't trying so hard to convince him the reefs were the single most important ecological system on the planet. Convince him that someone, mainly her, apparently, had to save them. In the pool he'd been able to tease her, get her to laugh and play as she got him ready for his first dive in an environment where he wouldn't drown if he forgot to turn his air tank on.

His knees slightly bent to absorb the shock of the waves, he moved with the deck as the boat bounced over the rough water. This was a beautiful vessel. They'd been heading straight out into the ocean for the past half hour, the blue water flying under the boat's hull, the sails taut in the crisp breeze. Laura was bringing him out to show him how exciting the ocean could be, but he seriously doubted it would be anywhere near as fun as standing here on the deck watching the horizon zoom by.

He glanced up to the front of the *Dancing Lady* where the captain had the wheel. While Laura apparently knew how to sail, this boat was too big for one person to handle. And she'd told him she used a crew when she went on diving expeditions, anyway.

Which made sense. It was pretty hard to keep track of a boat if you were a hundred feet down. And while anchors were a nifty thing, they weren't infallible. He could see where it would be a serious bummer to come up and find your boat had floated away. Particularly this far out. Nope, he was glad Captain Ted, a small, wiry man in his early forties, tanned to a deep brown by the Florida sun, and his one-man crew, Andre, a young college-age kid working on the boats to help pay his way through college, were on board. Even if that did mean he wasn't completely alone with Laura.

Actually, it was probably best they did have company. It would be easier for him to keep his hands where they belonged. Which meant anywhere that wasn't on Laura. As much as he wanted to touch her, as much as he wanted to quit playing games and get to the good stuff, she wasn't ready.

She was nervous about getting involved in something she knew would end soon. And since he didn't want any bad feelings on her part when he left, keeping his hands to himself was imperative. He watched her walk toward him now, dressed in the same white swimsuit she'd worn the day he met her, his fingers itching, his body aching.

She stepped up beside him, a frown marring her brow. "You're having fun, aren't you?"

He briefly thought about lying to her. She'd been so disappointed about how much fun he'd had talking boats with her dad and brothers at dinner the other night that she'd probably be a lot happier if she didn't know how much fun he was having at the moment. But he didn't like lying. Particularly to someone he wanted to take to bed. He nodded. "Yeah. I've never been on such a beautiful boat. Watching the sails catch the air, feeling the deck move beneath my feet, it's exhilarating."

She shook her head. "What is it about men and boats?"

"Hey, ladies like boats, too."

She shrugged. "Some of them."

"But you're not one of them."

"I wouldn't say that exactly. They're pretty essential to my job, after all. But they're workhorses to me. Nothing more."

"Blasphemy."

She chuckled. "Yeah, that's what my family thinks. But there it is. To me, that's what's beautiful." She pointed out to the water. "Look how rich a blue it is today."

He followed her gaze. The ocean was a deep, rich sapphire. And with the sun glinting off the waves' peaks, it was as sparkly and bright as the gem itself. He smiled, looking down at her. "All right, I almost believe that's your favorite color."

She smiled back at him, her hazel eyes twinkling. "You bet. Now, we're almost where we're going, so I'm going to go ahead and get the tanks on the BCs."

"Need some help?"

"Nah, I can get it. Enjoy yourself."

She moved down the deck to where fifteen or so air tanks were secured to the side rail. Turning from him, she lifted a tank from its holder, set it on the deck and then bent over to slide onto it the buoyancy control device—the BC—a nylon inflatable vest that allowed a diver to be neutrally buoyant.

His eyes popped open wide; heat poured through his system.

Bending over like she was, her long, tanned legs reaching toward the deck, her heart-shaped bottom poking out at him, the white material of her bathing suit stretching tight over those twin curves— Holy saints above. Forget about the ocean. Forget the damned boat. Heaven was right in front of him.

The camera around his neck burned.

He shouldn't.

He *really* shouldn't.

She'd kill him if she heard the shutter snap.

Then again…

Some things were worth dying for.

He raised the camera and clicked.

Twice.

She spun around, her gaze flying to him—and then the camera around his neck. Her eyes widened. "Did you just take a picture of my—my—" she sputtered, her cheeks turning bright pink. But outrage rapidly overtook embarrassment and her eyes narrowed into threatening little lasers. "Did you just take a picture of my butt?"

He held his hands up. "Now, Laura—"

"Don't 'now Laura' me. Did you or did you not just take a picture of my backside?"

He couldn't stop his smile. "Actually, I did. But it was only one."

Her eyes narrowed even more. "I distinctly heard the shutter click twice."

Busted. "Okay, two pictures. But—" He had to laugh. "Okay, I'm a chauvinistic pig. I admit it." He held his hands out from his sides. "Want to come beat me up? I promise to stand complacently while you exact restitution."

She held on to her glower for a full five seconds. Then she, too, laughed. "Brady, I swear to God if those pictures ever turn up anywhere public, you're a goner. For that matter, has it occurred to you how easy it would be for me to drown you while we're sixty feet down?''

''Well, actually, I hadn't thought of that.'' The fact that he thought the pictures would be worth dying for, he kept to himself.

''Well, I'd start thinking about it if I were you. One more picture like that and you're fish food.''

He held his hands up. ''Got it. No more pictures, I promise.'' At least ones she'd object to. He had every intention of taking dozens of others. Pictures of her he could pull out in the future and remember her by.

The boat suddenly slowed. He bent his knees to absorb the gentle rocking as it came to a halt. ''We're there?''

''So it would appear. Now, before we get dressed, I want to go over how it's going to work once we're in.''

''I'm listening.''

''Okay, we're going to tip backward over the side of the boat, just like we practiced at the pool. Your BC is going to be filled with air, so you're going to just pop back up on the surface like a cork once you've finished rolling over, right?''

''Yep.''

''Okay, once we're in, Andre is going to hand me a few things and then we're going to head to the bottom.''

He nodded. ''Hold the inflator hose for the BC over my head and press the release valve. As the air goes out of the BC, I'll sink to the bottom." He repeated the instructions he'd memorized and tried out at the pool.

"Right. Go as slow as you need to equalize your ears."

"Got it."

"Good. Now, there are no reefs on the bottom here, so what I want you to do is go straight to the ocean floor and settle on your knees."

Surprise washed through him. "No reefs?"

"Not today. Today we're just having a little fun. However, the fun I have planned requires that you pay close attention to the instructions I'm about to give you."

What could possibly require fancy instructions? Whatever it was, he hoped it was more fun than he'd had snorkeling the one time he'd tried out the sport. While he'd thought the reefs colorful and pretty, on the whole, he'd found the exercise seriously lacking in excitement. He forced his thoughts back to the moment at hand. "Okay, I'm listening."

Her expression turned serious. "Once you're settled on the bottom, it's imperative that you stay there. I don't want you swimming around. Just stay still and quiet. If we're lucky we'll be in for a great show."

His brow shot toward his hairline. "That's it? We're going to sit on the bottom of the ocean and wait for fish to come our way?"

She smiled, turning away and heading back to the

diving gear. "Trust me, you're going to have a great time. Very exciting."

Uh-huh.

"All righty, then, let's get dressed." She sat on one of the side benches and started pulling on her gear.

He followed suit and before he knew it they were sitting on the edge of the rail and then tipping into the big blue.

The cool water rushed over him as he fell backward into the ocean. Breathing from the tank of air on his back, he let the BC right him and pull him to the surface. Laura was right there, waiting for him when he popped up.

She pulled her regulator from her mouth. "Good job. You ready to go under?"

"Absolutely."

"Let me get my stuff." She swam to the boat where Andre handed her a big white bucket and long spear.

What was that for? She couldn't possibly have a little fishing planned, could she?

Nah. She didn't eat her friends. He couldn't imagine her stabbing them to death.

With her goodies in hand she turned back to him. "Let's go." She fitted her regulator back in her mouth, held the BC's inflator hose above her head, pushed the release button and disappeared under the surface.

He followed, the water closing over his head. The

first thing he noticed was the silence. Well, not silence exactly. He could hear the muted hiss of his regulator as he drew in a breath, the gurgle of the bubbles as he breathed out. But except for that there was an all-encompassing quiet as they descended slowly toward the white sandy bottom.

The occasional fish swam by, some big, some small. He turned slowly in the water, looking around. He could see for a fair distance, the murky edges an unmistakable reminder that the ocean went on practically forever in every direction. It was a bit eerie as he realized how big the ocean was and how little he was in it. A person could become totally lost down here. He glanced up at the surface, spying the bottom of the *Dancing Lady*. Good. It was still there.

A sudden noise filled the silence, and he realized the propeller on the *Dancing Lady* was spinning. Odd they hadn't used the motor on the way out here. They'd relied on the sails to get them here. So why the motor now? Was the *Dancing Lady* heading out? No. The anchor was still down. Was the revving motor a signal of some kind to return to the boat? He looked over to Laura, pointed toward the boat and lifted his shoulders, asking silently what was going on.

She shot him the diver's sign for okay and then pointed toward the ocean floor.

Apparently, the revving motor wasn't anything to worry about. He let a little more air out of his BC and continued his descent. He hadn't gone too much farther when Laura touched his shoulder and pointed out toward the edges of the ocean. A dark shadow moved at the far reaches of the murkiness.

A *big* dark shadow.

A thrill of excitement stole through his veins. Big fish would be cool. He wondered what they had out here. Swordfish? Marlin?

Sharks?

His heart beat a little quicker as the shadow got closer. Though a little heavier than he would have imagined, the dark silhouette did have that torpedo shape people associated with sharks. And it certainly moved like the sharks he'd seen on TV. But then, maybe every fish in the ocean moved like that.

Another shadow appeared on the hazy horizon, this one even bigger than the first.

Wow. Another shot of adrenaline shot through his system. He looked back to the first shape. It was closer now. A lot closer. Close enough for him to make out its grayish color, the telltale form of its nose and the unmistakable shape of its triangular dorsal fine. No doubt about it. Sharks.

Okay, this was exciting.

He slowly turned in the water as the first shark made a wide circle around them. It was huge, an easy ten feet long. And its girth reminded him of a sumo wrestler. But it looked a hundred times more agile than a wrestler. A hundred times more cunning. A thousand times more savage.

Getting his attention, Laura pointed to the ocean

floor. Right. He was supposed to settle on the bottom and watch the show. The idea of kneeling in the sand while eating machines swam over him was a little disconcerting. But then Laura was the expert here. If she said kneel on the ground, that was probably the safest place to be. Or was it?

She *had* mentioned feeding him to the fish. Nah, she was too good a sport for that. He let the rest of the air out of his BC, drifted the last ten feet to the bottom and settled awkwardly on his knees, the sand he disturbed swirling around him.

Laura settled much more gracefully about fifteen feet from him, barely disturbing the sand as she settled in. After setting the bucket next to her, she shot him the okay sign again, asking if he was okay.

He signed back, letting her know he was fine.

She pointed to the sea around them.

He glanced around again. There were five circling sharks now. One of them swam by so close he could have reached out and touched it, its raggedy teeth, those harbingers of death, all too visible as it glided by.

Oh, man.

The boat motor suddenly went quiet. Had the engine's revving been a call to the sharks? Maybe. In which case turning the roaring engine off was probably a good thing. They had plenty of company. He glanced back toward the murky edges. Two more shadows were headed their way.

His heart picked up a quick, steady tattoo, the

adrenaline flowing freely. He looked to Laura. She was keeping a sharp eye on the moving predators, but she looked calm, totally in control. She stuck the spear into the bucket she'd set in the sand next to her and made a quick stabbing motion. When she pulled it out, a big piece of cut up fish was stuck on the end.

One of the closer sharks made a quick turn toward her, its small yellow eyes locking on to the bait. Its big, heavy body hesitated, as if it were assessing the situation. And then it sprang into action with a flick of its powerful tail, swimming directly at Laura, its purpose clear.

That giant mouth opened and closed over the end of the spear. Laura held on with both hands as the shark thrashed its head, wrestling the meaty prize from the end of the spear. With another flick of its tail it raced off, the prize already halfway to its stomach.

Adrenaline poured through his system. Had he thought the ocean was a boring place? What was he thinking?

Laura stabbed another piece of fish and pulled it out of the bucket. Two sharks headed in her direction this time.

Images of shark frenzies he'd seen on TV flashed in his head. Fear streaked through him. He didn't want Laura caught in that mess. Not when the only reason she was here was to show him a good time.

He started to push off the bottom, hoping he could deflect the sharks before they zeroed in on her.

But at the last minute the bigger shark gave the other one a hard bump with its nose. The smaller shark veered off, moving back to the perimeter where the other sharks circled. The big shark hit the end of the spear like lightning, shook its head viciously and swam off with the prize.

Austin settled back on the bottom, the shot of fear easing off. Apparently, there was a pecking order here, one the sharks recognized and respected.

Laura speared another piece of fish, which rapidly disappeared into another gaping, sharp-toothed maw.

The shark swam by him, swallowing the big piece of fish whole, the muscles under his jaw working in a undulating gulp. The unbelievable power and girth of these animals was stunning. No, not animals. Fish. Somehow even more amazing.

Okay, he was damned impressed. But he'd sat on the bottom long enough. He wanted to play. He caught Laura's attention and pointed to his chest, asking if he could feed the next one.

She nodded, the bubbles from her regulator creating a ribbon pattern as they headed toward the surface.

When he started to swim in her direction, she held her hand out, indicating he should stay put. He settled back into the sand while she picked up the bucket, placed it in the same hand she held the spear in and swam in his direction.

The closest shark whipped around, heading straight for her.

Fear shot through him again. He tensed to spring into action. Though what the hell he thought he was going to do, he didn't know.

She merely flicked her free hand in front of the approaching shark's nose, like someone shooing a fly away.

The giant fish changed direction with lightning speed, swimming away.

Amazing.

She settled next to him, set the bucket down, speared a piece of fish and handed him the spear.

He'd barely taken hold of the spear when a shark streaked at him. Excitement tinged with the exhilarating power of fear pounded through him as that tooth-lined jaw opened before him.

Laura quickly straightened his elbows, pushing the spear farther away from his body, and closed her hands over his just as the shark hit.

And it was a good thing or the shark would have run off with the spear. He hadn't been prepared for the powerful shake of the fish's head. He watched the predator swim away with the chunk of fish, pure excitement racing through him. He'd just fed a shark. He turned back to Laura, holding the spear up, indicating he wanted to do it again.

She nodded her head, took the spear, loaded it with another piece of fish and handed it back to him.

He positioned it correctly this time and closed his hands tight.

Apparently she was happy with his hold because she made no attempt to help, but merely knelt quietly next to him.

Two sharks that had been swimming in tandem at the perimeter flicked their powerful tails in unison and came at him.

His heart rate kicked up another notch, but he didn't panic. He held tight, spear poised in front of him as the lethal monsters sped toward him.

There was no nudging this time, but at the last second one of the sharks veered off, leaving the other to snatch the bait. Two savage shakes of its head and it and the fish were gone. Adrenaline rocketing through his system, Austin held the spear out to Laura again.

She shrugged and tipped the bucket toward him. Empty.

Damn. Just when things were getting megafun. He held his thumb up, asking if they should head to the surface.

She held her index finger up, telling him to wait. And then held her hand up, indicating he should again stay where he was.

Fresh excitement wound through him. He didn't know what she had planned, but if it was anything like that last bit, he couldn't wait.

She took the spear from him and laid it carefully next to the bucket before she gently pushed off from the bottom and swam out to the perimeter where the sharks were circling. As one of the deadly predators swam by she reached out and let her hand glide over its gray body.

She was *petting* the shark. A tendril of apprehension ran through him. She didn't have anything to offer the fish in place of her own flesh this time. And she'd left the spear by him. She was out there, a lone human against seven of earth's most ruthless eating machines. Some of his excitement edged toward worry.

But she seemed completely at ease as she stayed where she was, floating in place, her gaze tracking the shark she'd just touched as it made its way around the perimeter. When it approached her again, she reached out. This time it seemed as if the shark adjusted his path to connect with her hand.

Okay, that was cool. Damned cool. But he had to admit this wasn't nearly as much fun as feeding the damned beasts. As a matter of fact, it was more nerve-racking than fun. And since he knew she was doing this just to impress him, he'd just as soon she stop. But he didn't know how to communicate that to her. He thought about swimming over, collecting her up and heading toward the surface, but she'd told him to stay put. For all he knew, sharks didn't like two humans swimming together. So he stayed glued to the bottom.

Though she kept an active eye on the other sharks swimming around her, she again tracked the shark she'd just petted around the circle. This time when the monster approached she placed herself right in his path.

Austin's heart stopped. What the hell was she doing now?

The shark slowed, its beady eyes watching Laura as sharply as she watched it.

His heart exploded into overtime. What the hell *was* she doing? Daring the damned monster to bite her?

Every instinct in his body told him to race to her and jerk her out of the shark's path, but he fought the urge, remaining locked in place, afraid even to breathe. The last thing he wanted to do was startle the beast. The eerie quiet of the ocean became even more so as bubbles quit rising from his regulator.

The shark's nose bumped into Laura's stomach.

The world stopped. Hadn't he read somewhere that sharks often bumped their victims before actually attacking them?

But this shark didn't bump and swim away, the way the articles said. He was staying put, his nose against her belly. Austin clenched his fists, using every ounce of willpower he had to stay put. The only thing keeping him there was the knowledge that she was the expert, not him. Hopefully, she knew what the hell she was doing. He wished she'd get the hell away from the predator.

But she didn't. She stayed still as the shark snuggled his nose tighter into her belly. And then she slowly reached forward with both hands and started stroking him behind his gills.

Fear exploded in Austin. Not the kind of fear that had sung through him only minutes before. That kind of fear energized him, made him feel he was truly alive. But there was nothing energizing about this fear. It was a sickening, writhing coil in the pit of his gut as he waited for the shark to get impatient, open his giant mouth and bite her in half.

Get the hell away from him, Laura! The words screamed in his head. But he couldn't say them. Not down here at the bottom of the ocean. Not with the regulator in his mouth and water all around them. Impotence poured through him. Impotence and guilt.

This was his fault. If he hadn't been such a pig-headed, arrogant ass about the article, if he'd taken more time to reassure her about it, if he'd just shown more interest in the damned thing, she wouldn't be down here trying to convince him the ocean was an exciting place.

He was breathing like a freight train now, the bubbles noisy in his ears. Not good. If he wasn't careful, if he didn't slow his breathing down, he'd probably suck his air tank dry in the next two minutes. And then where would he be? Wait a minute. If he was low on air...

Perfect.

He lifted his hand, slowly so as not to unsettle the shark, but high enough that Laura would hopefully notice.

She did, thankfully, her head slowly turning in his direction.

He clenched a fist and tapped it against his chest three times, the sign for "low on air."

She gave her head a slow nod, gently pulled her hands from the shark and with a subtle flip of her fins disengaged from him.

The shark remained motionless for a second longer, as if it were asleep, then moved on, his big body gliding effortlessly away.

Relief poured through Austin. At least until the next shark swam into his path of vision and he remembered they were in the middle of a pack of the deadly creatures. He held his thumb up, the sign for heading to the surface.

She nodded as she pointed to the gear beside him.

Yes, the spear. He grabbed the weapon, though realistically the idea of fending off one of these behemoths with the small spear was laughable. But at the moment, he'd take whatever advantage he could get. He handed the bucket off to her as they made their way up. He wanted his hands free to use the spear if need be.

The sharks' swimming pattern shifted, following them as they made their way to the top.

Great. Fresh fear coiled in his stomach. They still might not get out of this alive. *She* might not get out of this alive. His grip tightened on the spear. Yes, she would, dammit. And if they both got out of this alive he'd damn well make sure nothing like this ever happened again. He'd knuckle down and get to work. Hell, there wouldn't be a man on earth more interested in the reefs than he was. And he'd make sure Laura knew it. He'd write the best article of his career, dammit. If she just got out of this ocean in one piece.

They finally popped up on the surface.

Laura dropped the regulator from her mouth. "Give me the spear while you get your gear off and hand it to Andre."

He shook his head, his heart trying to pound its way out of his chest. "You get your gear off and get out of the water. Then I'll hand you the spear."

"This isn't the time to be macho, Brady. Now get going. This is the one moment when we're most vulnerable."

His fear flashed into anger. "You think I don't know that? Get up the damned ladder, Laura."

Her eyes popped wide at his sudden outburst. But she didn't waste any more time talking. She swam quickly to the ladder, efficiently removed her fins, tossed them up to Andre, slipped out of her BC, handed it up and scampered up the metal rungs.

She was safe.

Now all he had to do was get his sorry ass out before one of the shadows swimming right under his feet tipped their heads up and took a giant bite. He swam to the ladder and handed the spear up. Andre took it and leaned over the rail, his gaze fixed on the ocean around Austin while Laura waited for him to hand his gear up. He removed his equipment as quickly as his novice abilities allowed and tossed them up. Then he raced up the ladder, breathing a little sigh of relief as his toes cleared the waves. But the minute his feet hit the deck, he exploded, rounding on Laura. "What the *hell* were you doing down there?"

She rocked back at his attack. "What are you mad about? You thought the ocean was a boring place. I just wanted to show you it wasn't."

Fresh guilt slashed at him, pushing his temper up another notch. "I didn't tell you to offer yourself up as *bait*, for crying out loud."

Her brows arched and she glanced at Andre, then back to him. "Maybe we should take this below?"

He didn't care if the whole world heard, but she was already heading down the narrow, steep stairs that led to the below deck quarters.

He followed her down to the teak-paneled salon with its small table and leather seating areas.

She strode across the room and spun back toward him. "What is wrong with you?"

"What's wrong with *me*? What's wrong with *you*? Letting that animal stick its nose in your stomach. Have you lost your mind?"

She shook her head indignantly, drops of water shaking loose from her wet hair. "It wasn't some wild idea I cooked up on the spur of the moment. I've done it before."

"That doesn't make me feel better, Laura."

She rolled her eyes. "I was in control. Noth—"

"The hell you were. Those aren't trained circus animals. They're wild, carnivorous beasts. With an occasional taste for human flesh. And *you* snuggled right up next to one so all he had to do was open his mouth to get some." He stabbed his fingers through his hair, just thinking of it.

Surprise flashed across her face. Followed by an unholy gleam of smugness. "Were you scared? Big, bad, thrill-a-minute, Brady? Scared?"

Torture wouldn't drag that truth from his lips. "Don't be ridiculous."

But she knew he was lying; he could see the knowing look in her gaze. Mischief sparkled in her eyes, and an evil smiled turned her lips. "Now who's lying?"

"Not me."

She cocked a delicate brow. "No? Good. Because next time I thought we might try riding them. They don't like it nearly as well, but if you're looking for excitement…"

He narrowed his eyes in warning. "Shut up, Laura." She was teasing, but it wasn't funny. Not to him. He could still see that shark snuggled up to her. Still feel the fear writhing in his gut.

Her evil smile got a little broader. "Come on, think of the tale that would make. You could bring your camera, take a picture of me holding on to one of their dorsal fins."

His gut clenched. "Last warning."

She chuckled, having far too much fun at his expense. ''Or if that's not exciting enough for you, we could travel Down Under. Hit the Great Barrier Reef. Look up some great whites. You'll love them. Three times as big as the guys out there. Great big ol' mouths.'' She held her hands three feet apart, showing the size of the great white's bite.

That was it. He strode over to her and grabbed her by the shoulders, his fingers itching to shake her into silence. But violence wasn't an option. An evil smile of his own pulled at his lips. There was more than one way to quiet a lady.

He closed his mouth over hers.

Laura froze as Brady's lips crashed down on hers, hard and hot and a little bit angry.

She'd obviously pushed her teasing a little too far. She should definitely push him away.

But when she put her hands on his shoulders, pushing wasn't what they did. Her fingers clamped onto his skin, and she leaned forward into his hard, wet body.

His hands tightened on her shoulders, pulling her closer still, his wet skin sliding against her, his lips crushing hers.

Oh God, how long had it been since she'd been kissed?

Too long.

And she'd never been kissed like this. This was no polite kiss orchestrated to convince her that he was the man for her. No see-how-nice-I'll-treat-you kiss. This was a raw, primal, sit-up-and-pay-attention kiss.

She could get lost in this kiss.

She pushed up on her toes, opening her mouth, taking him in.

His tongue invaded her mouth, hot and angry.

But his anger didn't last long. The passion that had been sparking between them since the day he'd first shown up on her lawn rapidly took over.

Her tummy wasn't tingling now. It was buzzing with need.

She pressed against him, reveling in the feel of his wet skin against hers, her nipples peaking, goose bumps racing over her skin. She ran her hands down his arms and then back up to his head, plowing her fingers through his wet hair, urging him to kiss her deeper.

A greedy moan vibrated in his throat, and he grabbed her hips, bringing her tight up against him, the hard ridge of his arousal pressing into her.

Sensations she'd never felt before raced through her. Heat and need and an ache so deep she didn't know how to appease it. As if of their own volition, her hips lifted against his. Oh yeah. That was it. Her fingers dug into his hair. A whimper sounded in her throat.

He walked her back until she hit the wall, his mouth never leaving hers, his hands keeping their hips locked together. With the wall behind her, allowing their hips to stay locked together, he moved his hands up her ribs, his fingers tracing her curves until they came to her breasts.

Hot waves of need exploded in her as his hands closed over the sensitive flesh. It had been so long since she'd let a man touch her like this, she'd forgotten what it felt like. No, she hadn't. It had *never* felt like this. The few men she'd ever let touch her breasts had touched her with the same practiced restraint they'd used when they'd kissed her. There was nothing restrained about Brady's touch. Nothing restrained about Brady at all.

His fingers were greedy, his mouth ravenous and his hips...

Oh man. With nothing but their swimsuits between them, his hard length sent a giddy thrill and wave after wave of tingling need through her.

He pulled his lips from hers and kissed his way down her throat, tasting and nipping as he moved lower and lower until his hot mouth closed over the wet material covering her nipple.

Fire slashed through her. She rocked her head against the wall, a soft moan vibrating in her throat. No man had ever kissed her there before.

He suckled, his lips hot against the cool wetness of her suit.

Just when she thought her world might explode, he stopped, pulling his lips from her. His breathing heavy, he straightened, leaning his head against her collarbone. ''We've got to slow down.''

Her fingers tightened in his hair. "I don't want to slow down."

"If we don't slow down, this is going to be over before we even realize it's started."

The reality of his words washed over like a cold shower. "Oh God, what am I saying? We can't do this."

His head snapped up as if she'd shot him, his intense, heated gaze locking on to hers. "Trust me, we can do this."

She laughed, a hoarse, pitiful sound. "No, we can't. *I* can't."

He dropped his head against the wall next to hers, his rapid breath tickling her ear, his hands dropping to her hips. "Laura—"

"I don't even know your middle name."

His fingers tightened on her hips, his erection pressed against her. "Scott. My middle name's Scott."

Another strained laugh fell from her lips. "You don't know mine."

"What is it?"

Lynn. It hovered on the tip of her tongue. But while this might not be such a big thing for Brady— he'd made it clear he'd had lovers before—it was a big thing for her. She wanted to know the first man she took as a lover. Really know him. And she wanted more than a hard, quick coupling in the bottom of a boat.

Summoning all the strength she had, she gently pushed him away and shook her head. "I can't tell you. Not yet."

Eight

Austin lay on Laura's leather sofa, staring up at the ceiling. Again. No way was he going to get any sleep tonight, either. Not only was it still hotter than Satan's lair, but after that little make-out session this afternoon, neither his body nor his imagination was going to let him anywhere near unconsciousness. And if the sound of Laura flopping around in her bed meant anything, she was having the same trouble.

"Laura."

The rustling sheets suddenly stilled.

He smiled at the moonlit ceiling. "I know you're awake. I can hear you flopping around."

Still no answer. Shaking his head at her stubbornness, he pushed up from the sofa and padded over to her bedroom door where he leaned against the jamb. "Come on, Laura. Talk to me."

She was lying on her side dressed in a pair of old lightweight, short-sleeved summer pajamas, a sheet pulled up to her waist, the moonlight washing over her.

He stood quietly for a moment, just watching her pretend to sleep. She was so beautiful. With her silky hair in disarray, her eyelashes shadowing her cheekbones, those bee-stung lips highlighted by the moon's silvery light, she was the image of every erotic thought he'd ever had. He wanted to stride across the room, run his fingers through her hair, kiss her soft cheeks, ravish those lips.

He smiled in the darkness. Ravish. What a ridiculous word. But pretty damned accurate. Which was why he needed to put an end to her charade before he gave in to those wants. He sighed. "You faker. Should I come nudge you?"

Her eyes flew open, and she whipped around, holding her hand out to keep him where he was. "No. I'm awake."

He chuckled. "I know."

She shifted onto her back, stretching one leg out straight and cocking the other off to the side as she ran a distracted hand through her hair, pushing a few stray strands out of her face. "I don't think these midnight chats are the best idea."

Arm still over her head, she arched her back, stretching. The move plumped her breasts nicely, their soft, enticing forms pushing against her pajamas. Heat stole through him as his gaze slid lower to the place where the sheet dipped in the triangle created by her cocked knee and her straight one. It wouldn't take much for a man to push the other knee aside, make room for himself in that heavenly triangle.

Blood poured to his groin. "If you don't think these chats are a good idea, want to hear my other ideas for the night?'' His voice was as rough as the erotic thoughts pounding in his head.

''*No.*'' She snapped up, scooting against the head-board and pulling her knees up against her chest.

Luckily the lower half of his body was in deep shadow, easily dark enough to hide his arousal. Otherwise, she'd probably go screaming from the room. ''Too bad. It might have been fun.''

She shot him a warning scowl as she tossed her pillows behind her back. ''Stop it, or I'll boot you out of here.''

He didn't want that so he changed the subject to something more serious. Something he'd been wondering about since she'd snuggled up to that shark this afternoon. ''Why is this article so important to you?''

Her gaze flitted away from his and she shrugged. ''It just is.''

''That's not an answer.''

She laughed softly. ''I know. But it's the only one you're going to get.''

''Too personal?''

''Maybe.''

''I'll take that as a yes.'' And the yes was disappointing. He wanted her to let him in, to consider him a confidant. Which was damned silly. He'd never wanted any of the women he'd slept with in the past to consider him such. So why did he want that with Laura?

''You should go back to your sofa, Brady. Try to get some sleep.''

He snorted. ''Like we're going to sleep, anyway.''

She plowed her fingers through her hair. ''You're right. What do you want to talk about?''

He smiled. ''We could talk about what happened in the boat this afternoon.''

She shook her head adamantly. ''Oh, no. This night is already hot enough. I am not going to tease myself into a frenzy on top of it by thinking about that.''

Well, that sounded damned promising. ''So you were...having fun?''

She looked at him as if he'd lost his mind. ''Duh, Brady. You scorched my toes. You kiss like... like...'' A delicate shiver ran through her body.

A little thrill of pleasure stole through him. ''Yeah, how do I kiss?''

She shook her head. ''Another thing I'm not going to do is sit here and stroke your ego, get us both more hot and bothered so we can spend the rest of the night with our nerves pounding like tidal waves.''

''Tossing and turning could be fun. If we did it together.''

She chuckled, shaking her head. ''Stop it already.'' She pulled the top drawer open on her nightstand and pulled out what looked like a small yellow blanket.

''What's that?''

"A baby blanket for my soon-to-be niece or nephew." Leaning over, she picked up a toaster-sized basket from the floor.

"Seth's baby?"

She nodded.

His body back in control, he pushed away from the door and strode over to the bed. The basket was full of needles and little coils of colorful threads. "What are you doing? Sewing something on it?"

She turned the blanket around and held it up. "A little scene for the baby."

He smiled. "A picture of the reefs. Of course."

"Hey, they're wallpapering the poor kid's room with sailboats. If I'm going to save him, I've got to do it early."

He chuckled, sitting on the edge of her bed by her feet. As he did so, his gaze caught on a stack of small blankets folded in the open space that made up the bottom half of the nightstand. He picked the top one up, holding it open. This one was light blue rather than yellow, but the motif was the same. It was a picture of the reefs. "You making him—or her—more than one?"

"Nope, that's for my cousin Honey's baby. He or she is due just before the regatta. I finished it up the other day, but I haven't had time to mail it yet."

"Yeah? What about the others? It looks like your family is having a population explosion."

She laughed. "We are."

He stared at the blanket in his hands. At the colorful rendition of the reefs. At the tiny stitches she'd applied one at a time. It was a lot of work. A whole lot of work. There had to be hundreds, maybe thousands, of stitches on the blanket. And there was a whole stack of them in her nightstand.

Her foot bumped his thigh. "What's that odd look for?"

He shifted his gaze to her. "I don't know. It just seems like an awful lot of work for a baby who's going to just throw up on the thing."

She laughed. "They're washable."

"Yeah, but still. I mean, realistically the kid's never going to know you put all this work into it. And the pictures aren't going to mean anything. They're just going to be colors to the kid."

"Oh, I don't know. We don't really know when images start imprinting on kids' minds. It might very well be from the day they start seeing. And if it is, and if one of the first things the child sees is a picture of the reef, a picture of a fish, and he becomes a little more attached to his natural environment because of it, how great is that? And besides, it's not really about the picture. I love the reefs so, yes, I'd like to share that with the babies in the family. But it's not about the picture. It's about the…I don't know, the care and love that goes into the effort. I want the babies to know I care about them."

"The blankets will be long gone before the kids have that kind of cognitive ability."

She rolled her eyes, smiling. "Maybe not some of these kids."

"What does that mean?"

She waved away the question. "Nothing. But cognitive ability doesn't have anything to do with it. A child doesn't have to be old enough to know what words like love and caring mean to know if he or she has those things. From the moment they're born, they know if they're surrounded by care or indifference. Their little hearts know, Brady. Their little hearts know."

A place suspiciously close to his own heart ached. A gaping, dark, empty place. Maybe she was right. He'd certainly known he hadn't had either of those things long before he'd been able to put it into words.

What would it be like to have a woman like Laura in his life? Someone who loved those around her so strongly. Someone who cared for those around her. What would it be like to feel just a hint of those emotions? Even for a little while?

He reached out and gently ran his finger down her arm. Goose bumps broke out on her skin, and her nipples peaked beneath her soft pajamas. "I want us to be together, Laura. I wanted it the first moment I saw you. And I want it now." Even more. So much more.

She looked at him, longing and trepidation in her eyes. "Do you really think we know each other well enough to be jumping into bed together?"

"This isn't rocket science, Laura. I know I want

you.'' He lowered his gaze to her nipples. ''I think you want me. What else is there to know?''

She smiled, a shy, thoughtful smile. ''That's the question, isn't it? And I'm not sure I have the answer yet.''

Damn. He pushed up from her bed. ''Okay. But whatever it is you think you need to know, find it, will you? You're wasting time.'' Time that was far, far too valuable to waste.

At least to him.

Two days later, Laura sat on her sofa with the magazines she'd picked up from the library strewn around her. Magazines carrying Austin Brady's articles. It was a beautiful Saturday morning and she was enjoying it thoroughly. The late morning sun was making its way up her windows. A bit of a cross breeze blew in the front door and out the back, riffling the occasional shiny page. And she was discovering all kinds of things about the man who was currently sharing her house. A prudent move considering his relentless push and her own less-than-chaste response.

She'd already read several of the pieces. They were good. Damned good. The man was clever with words. But while his style lent panache to his stories, it was their heart that captured her attention. After Brady had told her he preferred assignments with a spark of excitement she'd expected to find the articles filled with details like the rush of snow hitting his face, the skin-searing heat of flame or the peculiar snap bullets made when they whizzed by his head. But while there was the occasional reference to such adrenaline-spiking events, they were not the focus of his articles.

She tossed the magazine down to the finished pile and grabbed another one from the to-be-read stack. She opened the periodical to the table of contents and glanced down, looking for his byline. There it was. "Rwanda: A Shameful Civil War" by Austin Brady.

Another war story. He did seem to gravitate in that direction. But his articles weren't so much about the soldiers and guns and fighting as they were about the innocent civilians who got caught in the middle of a dictator's or local warlord's ambitions. It was an interesting, heart-wrenching slant. One she hadn't anticipated a thrill seeker to take.

The screen door slammed behind her and Austin's footsteps sounded on her tile floor. "Come on, put those dusty things away and come out and play."

She chuckled, glancing over her shoulder. "Not yet. I'm reading. Come sit with me."

He strode over to the sofa and plopped down at the opposite end from her, the only area that wasn't covered in magazines. A few of the magazines slid into his thigh as the leather cushion gave under his weight. He picked one up, glancing at the cover. "Oh jeez, Laura. This thing's ten years old."

"So?"

"So I write better than that now." He tossed the magazine off the end of the couch, out of her reach.

She smiled, shaking her head. "I've already read that magazine. It's too late to hide it. And I liked the article."

"I didn't say it was bad. I just said the more recent stuff is better."

She smiled, shaking her head. "You are so vain."

He shot her an outraged look. "I am no such thing."

She laughed. "Yes you are. And arrogant, too. But that's okay, I kind of like those things about you."

He rolled his eyes, slouching back against the sofa. "Gee, thanks."

"You're welcome." She laughed again, opening the magazine to the Rwanda article. A young black boy with the biggest eyes she'd ever seen stared up from the page. "What a sad little boy."

He glanced over at the magazine, his mouth turning down as he spied the picture. "He *was* a sad little boy. A devastated little boy. Three weeks before I got there some butcher had killed his father and cut his mother's hands off. Anatole was the oldest of six kids. He didn't know how to take care of his mother or how to feed himself and his brothers and sisters."

"Oh God, what did you do?" She knew instinctively he had done something.

But he shook his head, his expression bleak. "There wasn't much I could do. I gave them what food supplies I had—damned few, I might add—and the stash of painkillers and antibiotics I always carry with me when I travel. Took his picture. Wrote the article and prayed someone somewhere who could really do something was paying attention.''

She stared at the picture and the caption next to it. *Anatole, one of the lucky survivors of the genocide.* She ran her finger over the picture, thinking. ''You remember his name. Even today.''

''Of course I remember his name.''

She checked the date of the magazine. ''This is a pretty old article. There must have been a lot of little children since. A lot of people and names.''

''Thousands.''

''And you remember all their names?''

''Not all of them. The adults' names slip away sometimes. But I remember all the children's names. They never go away.''

Something clicked in her brain. A key piece of information about Austin Brady. She looked up from the magazine. ''It's about the children, isn't it?''

He raised a questioning brow. ''What's about the children?''

''Your articles. They're about the children.'' She shook her head. ''No, more than that. They're not *about* the children. They're cries of help *for* the children. That's why you write them.''

He grimaced, a hint of red flushing his tanned cheeks. ''You're reading way too much into it.''

She shook her head, watching him. ''I don't think

so. I think your childhood was bumpy, and now you're trying to improve the lives of other kids.''

He all but rolled his eyes. ''It's obvious your degree *isn't* in psychology. My childhood was a cakewalk compared to these kids.''

''Maybe. But that doesn't negate my theory.''

He frowned, clearly unhappy with the subject matter. ''I would be willing to bet most of us have some dysfunction in our families. Your mother still serves you seafood, for crying out loud, which from what I observed the other night, makes you most unhappy. But that unhappiness hasn't made you want to go out and save the world.''

She smiled, wondering why he was so uncomfortable with her thinking he was doing a good thing. Maybe he thought it didn't fit with his thrill-a-minute reputation. Whatever his reason, she wouldn't press the point. She was pretty sure she had a handle on the truth. And that was all that mattered. ''No, my mother's penchant for serving lobster when I'm there hasn't made me want to save the world. But I have to admit, I hadn't thought of it as dysfunctional before, just annoying. Do you think it's dysfunctional? Like some kind of passive-aggressive thing?''

''I don't know. Do you?''

She shrugged. ''Maybe. I'll have to think about it. In the meantime, tell me about your mom. What was she like?''

He frowned. ''My mother was a very sad woman.''

She cocked her head, studying him. "Why?"

"Because she loved my father and he didn't love her back."

"No?" He'd hinted as much earlier. But she wanted more details now.

He shook his head, his lips turning down in disgust. "No. In fact, the only person Jack Brady ever loved was himself. The only thing he ever cared about was making himself happy. And what made him happy was bright lights, fast women and gambling."

She raised a brow. "Gambling?" No wonder there hadn't been enough money for food.

"Yep. He was a Las Vegas boy. Came home just often enough to keep my mom thinking maybe he'd come home for good someday."

"But he never did?"

He shook his head. "Ironically, he came home a little more often after she died. Not much, but maybe enough that it would have made a difference. Made her happy."

Her heart squeezed. "What did she die of?"

"She went out to pick up a bottle of sleeping pills one day and a drunk driver hit her."

"Oh God, Brady. I'm sorry."

He shrugged a shoulder as if trying to make her believe, or maybe to help himself believe, that he was over the loss now.

She didn't know if that made it better or worse. "How old were you?"

"Seventeen. My last year of high school."

"Seventeen," she whispered, reading between the lines. "Seventeen, and your dad only came home a little more often? Did you move in with relatives?"

He laughed a humorless sound. "There weren't any relatives. My dad and mom were both estranged from their families. After the accident it was just me and good old dad." There was such bitterness in his voice.

"He still left you alone sometimes?"

"More often than not. But that suited us both. By then I had no illusions about who my father was— or how he felt about me. And I blamed him for my mother's death. After all, she was out buying the pills she needed to forget that her husband wasn't at home where he belonged. It was much more comfortable when he wasn't around."

"But it must have been lonely." She pictured a seventeen-year-old boy, on the cusp of manhood, yes, but still, just a child, knocking around an empty house after the unexpected death of his mother.

He shrugged again. "Like I said, my mother was a sad woman. And as I mentioned, she had a habit of drowning her sorrows in alcohol and pills. Even when she was alive, it was a quiet house."

It was a sad picture. One that made her believe even more strongly that when he headed off to his war zones, camera in hand, he had a mission in mind. One lonely little boy who'd suffered through his own loss, hoping to help a few others through their own difficult fate. She traced her finger over Anatole's sad, desperate expression. "Did you ever get any political response from your articles? Did someone who could make a real difference pick up the cause?"

"Sometimes. But never enough."

No, there never seemed to be enough aid for the troubled spots of the world. But he'd made a difference. That was what counted.

He picked up another magazine and tossed it onto the coffee table. "So if you don't want to come out and play, I can think of some interesting things we could do in here." His tone made it clear he was thinking sweaty bodies and twisted sheets.

She smiled, shaking her head. "You're relentless."

"I have to be. You're stubborn."

"I'm not ready yet."

He sighed in frustration. "Is this the middle-name thing again? Because I've already told you mine and I could certainly call your mom and ask her yours."

Wanting to know his middle name had been about learning who he was. The articles strewn around her had solved that dilemma. Solved the dilemma *and* made the man more tempting. "It's not the name thing."

"Then what is it?"

"I don't know." She only knew she wasn't ready.

"You're killing me, you know that?"

She smiled at the little-boy whine. "You'll live."

"I might not. Men have died of broken hearts."

"We're not talking about your heart, we're talking about your—"

He held his hand up. "No talking dirty. I can't take the titillation."

She laughed. "If it's any consolation, I think we're getting closer."

Hope sparked in his eyes. "Yeah? Any idea when we might actually get there?"

She didn't have a clue, because she didn't know what was stopping her from falling into bed with him. It certainly wasn't lack of sexual chemistry. Or even emotional chemistry. Those things were there. They liked each other, were definitely attracted to each other. And yet, something was missing. Something important.

And while she didn't know what it was, she was certain she would know it when she found it. She gave him a smile, ignoring the need she felt just looking at the man. "I'll let you know."

Nine

Laura made her way down the crushed-shell path to her parents' private docks. She and Brady had just pulled up to her parents' house a few minutes ago. While he went in to talk to her dad about setting up a day to see the boatyards, she'd decided to head on down to the docks and get the *Dancing Lady* ready for today's outing.

She smiled at the bright pink and white hibiscus blooming along the narrow trail. She loved this narrow walk with its hibiscus and palms doing their best to crowd each other out. But then today she loved everything. She was taking Brady out for his first dive along the reefs so he could take pictures for the article he'd been busily writhing over the last few days. She couldn't wait to show him her favorite part of the world.

She had to give the guy credit. Since the shark incident he'd been nothing but attentive when it came to the article. Which was not to say she'd seen any real interest in his eyes when she went over facts and figures at the lab. But he was paying attention, which was nice, particularly since she knew he was doing it simply because it was important to her.

As she headed farther down the path, voices drifted up from the docks. Her father's and, she thought, Seth's. She smiled. Since Brady obviously wasn't going to find her father at the house, he'd be along shortly. Good. She liked having him with her. Liked the way he made her want to smile all the time. Liked the sexual energy that hummed between them.

As she got closer to the wharf the words became clearer. "What did Gretchen say?" her father asked, the words slightly muffled as they made their way through the thick vegetation lining the path.

Gretchen? One of Marcus's Protean sisters was named Gretchen. Laura's steps slowed and she listened closer.

"She said she found tracks indicating a hacker had made his way into our computers at Evans Yachts," Seth answered.

This was no casual conversation. She paused, her mind whirring with questions. What was Gretchen doing checking out the computer systems at Evans Yachts? Didn't she live on Brunhia? And who was trying to hack into the computers at Evans Yachts? No doubt if she strode onto the wharf and asked, they'd tell her it was the mystery person looking for the specs on Holt's boat. Well, she wasn't going to give them a chance to lie to her today. She was still a couple curves back from the docks where they couldn't see her. She held her ground, listening.

"I thought you had Gideon put up new firewalls." That was Holt's voice.

"Apparently someone got through them," Seth said.

"Did they get anything?" her dad asked, his voice tight, worried.

"She wasn't sure at first, but…"

"But what?" Holt pushed.

"But then she was able to track the hacker back to his computer. What she found there indicated whoever stuck his fingers in our pie knows about the meeting we have planned for the regatta."

"The meeting with the navy?" Urgency sounded in her father's voice.

"Yes," Seth affirmed.

The *navy?* What on earth did Evans Yachts have to do with the navy? Laura cocked her head, listening closer.

"Dammit, that means we have a traitor somewhere," said her father. "Either at Evans Yachts or in the navy."

A *traitor?* Not a thief or a spy. A traitor. That sounded big time.

"Hey, are you waiting for me?"

Laura jumped at Brady's voice as he made his way down the path from the house. She'd been listening so hard to the conversation on the dock that she hadn't heard him coming along. She quickly turned to him, holding her finger to her lips. "Shh."

But her warning was too late. There was already a flurry of voices on the dock and footsteps heading their way. Damn.

Her father led the pack as he came around the sharp turn in front of her, Seth and Holt on his heels. "Laura. I wasn't expecting you today." His expression was all sunshine and brightness, but tension radiated from his body.

"I called Mom earlier this morning to tell her we'd be over for the *Dancing Lady*. Apparently she forgot to tell you."

Her father's lips tightened. "Apparently she did. The *Dancing Lady*'s down there. You're free to take her if you like." He waved a hand toward the docks, managing to force a smile back to his lips, pretending—hoping, no doubt—that she hadn't heard anything.

She rocked back on her heels, shaking her head. "Sorry, Dad. It's not going to be that easy. I want to know what's going on. And we're going to stand here until I do."

He sighed, a sharp, irritated sound designed more to make her back off than anything else. "I told you the other night at dinner what was going on. Someone's trying to get the specs on Holt's boat."

She gave a short, humorless laugh. "Yeah, right. I'm supposed to believe you've brought in Gretchen for that?"

Her father stilled, his gaze flashing to Brady, then back to her.

Belatedly she remembered his profession. Did she want him to hear this conversation? Just the other night she'd been worried about him discovering who the Proteans were.

But she knew him better now. Knew that people's feelings were important to him. Knew how important *children's* feelings were to him. Gretchen and Kurt had a beautiful little girl named Violet, just six months old now. Marcus's wife, Samantha, had given birth to their first child, a son they called Hank. Faith and Luke had just had a little boy. Gideon's wife Brooke was pregnant. Even if Brady thought the adults could handle the exposure, he wouldn't risk hurting their children. She was positive of it. Nothing they said here would make the papers. And right now it would be nice to have someone on her side.

She took a step back, aligning herself with Brady. "If you wanted to have this conversation in private, Dad, we should have had it a long time ago. Now we're going to do it my way. And I want Brady here."

As if sensing she needed a little support, Brady put his hand on her shoulder, giving it a reassuring squeeze.

She lifted up her chin and narrowed her gaze on her father. "Now, tell me why Gretchen's here. And don't try to tell me you've brought in another Protean just to foil someone who wants the specs on the *Unicorn.* I'm not going to buy it. Gretchen has a husband in Brunhia, and a six-month-old baby to take care of. You wouldn't have pulled her away if this wasn't urgent. And then, of course, there's the navy. Surely you're not going to try to convince me *they're* helping protect Holt's boat.''

Her father looked away, hands on his hips, a deep frown furrowing his brow.

But it was the obstinate press of his lips that caught her attention when he looked back. Despite what she'd heard, he still had no intention of telling her anything. She looked to Seth. He was wearing the same closed expression.

She turned to Holt, her last port in the storm. ''Come on, baby brother, spill it.''

He looked at their father and then at Seth, his feelings with the situation clearly written on his face. ''This is ridiculous. Tell her what's going on.''

Both her father and Seth gave him warning looks.

For several seconds the men of her family stared at one another, tension vibrating in the air. Finally Holt looked back to her, his lips pressed into a hard, thin line. ''We're building an innovative sub for the navy. And Rebelia's dictator is trying to steal the plans for it.''

''Oh, my God.'' Her mind whirred. ''A *sub?*''

Brady's hand tightened on her shoulder.

Her father and Seth scowled at Holt, promising retribution as soon as this discussion was over.

Silence filled the narrow path.

A thousand questions filled her head. She shook it, trying to make sense of what she'd heard. ''Since when does Evans Yachts build submarines?''

Her father cast another glance at Brady, but when

she didn't offer to ask him to leave, and when Brady stayed firmly rooted behind her, her father answered her question. "Seth got the idea for the Stingray about a year ago. And was making damned decent progress on it, too."

"But when I brought Gideon on board things started really picking up," Seth continued. "We've made amazing progress these past few months."

Betrayal slashed through her. They were building a sub. Something new and exciting and important. They'd brought in outsiders to help, but they'd kept her out of the loop. She tapped an angry foot. "Ah yes, Gideon. Super Technology Boy. I should have suspected there was more afoot than yacht building when you brought him on board."

"No reason you should have," Seth said. "I fully intend to use him for building yachts, too. The fastest in the industry."

"I'm sure you do. But we're talking about subs now. The ones darling little dictator DeBruzkya is after, apparently. Like he hasn't caused this family enough problems." She thought of the scary time Marcus and his wife Samantha had had with the crazy dictator. And then another thought popped into her head. "Wait a minute. That's why you perked up so much when you heard Brady had been to Rebelia, isn't it? You wondered if he was one of DeBruzkya's men."

Her father grimaced. "The thought occurred to us."

Angry on Brady's behalf, she tipped her chin up another notch. "He's not."

"We know he's not. We had Marcus check with his contacts in navy intelligence. Brady's clean."

Her mind jumped to the next conclusion. "Did you have Michaels checked out, too?"

A muscle in his jaw ticked. "Yes."

Of course he had. "What? You don't think your daughter's important enough to merit a magazine article on her own? There has to be an ulterior motive behind it? Some crazy dictator trying to infiltrate the Evans clan?" She shook her head in disgust. "In your mind it always comes down to the boats, doesn't it? Nothing else in the world could possibly be important."

Impatience and anger flashed in her father's eyes. "Don't be ridiculous. I didn't have the reporters checked out because I thought the article was bogus. I had them checked out to make sure you were safe. With all the other odd events going on—as you pointed out—it didn't seem implausible to me that DeBruzkya might use the article as a means to put someone close to you. I wanted to make sure that didn't happen."

"Yeah, right." She shoved aside the pain and hurt and concentrated on the task at hand: finding out exactly what was going on at Evans Yachts. "So why did you bring Gretchen in?"

"Gideon thought encrypting the computer files on the Stingray was a good idea."

"And who better to do that than Super Puzzle Girl. What about Drew's nontourists the other day? What's really going on there?"

Her father's expression got a little darker. "They're Rebelian spies, apparently. Scoping out the boatyard and offices."

She shook her head in disbelief. "And no one thought I should know? No one thought I should be keeping my eyes open for nefarious characters?"

"As long as you didn't know anything, you weren't a target," her father said.

"You don't seriously believe that, do you?"

"Yes, I do."

"Well, I don't believe it. I don't believe I'm not a target just because I don't work in the company. And I don't think my safety is the real reason, or at least the only reason, you kept everything a secret from me. I think part of your strategy is to keep me out of the loop so I'll feel isolated. So I'll quit my job at the institute and come to work at Evans Yachts, just to know what's going on."

Guilt darkened her father's expression, and he looked away. "That's what your mother thinks, too."

Her stomach clenched. "Is she right? Am *I* right?"

His brows snapped together and he looked away. "I don't know."

Pain curled through her. "Well, you had better start figuring it out, Dad. I'm tired of the emotional blackmail. Either I'm part of this family or I'm not."

Holt stepped toward her, his hand outstretched. "No one's trying to tell you that you don't belong in the family."

"Dad's message is loud and clear. If I'm not part of the business, I'm not part of the family."

Her father's gaze swung to hers. "I never said any such thing."

"Maybe not. But you certainly implied it." She drew a deep breath, trying to keep her emotions from spiraling out of control. She didn't want this to turn into a screaming match. "Look, I'm proud that my family builds the best boats in the world. I'm proud they've supported this country by building military boats in the past. I'm proud they're working on a new sub that can help keep us safe. But boats aren't what I do. I've chosen a profession. I'm sorry it's not the one you would have picked for me, but I'm happy with it. I'm *good* at it. And if that's not good enough for you…"

She ran a shaky hand through her hair. "You need to let me know, Dad, because I'm not going to spend the rest of my life fighting for a spot in this family. Either I belong or I don't." She motioned toward the dock, wanting nothing more than to get away. "Is there a captain down there who can run the boat for us?"

His expression brooding, her father said, "Ted and Andre are down on the *Pisces*. Holler at them."

The *Pisces* was her father's big luxury yacht. There was almost always crew on it. "Fine." Without another word she strode off, Brady behind her.

Ten

"You okay?" Austin asked as the *Dancing Lady* got underway, her white sails billowing in the wind.

Laura was leaning on the rail, staring out at the ocean, looking raw and...a little lost.

He moved closer to her, his shoulder brushing hers, letting her know she wasn't alone.

She managed a smile. "I'm fine. Sorry about that scene. You shouldn't have had to listen to that."

"Not a problem. I'm sorry you had to go through it."

She grimaced. "It's long overdue. I love my dad dearly, but at some point he has to realize I've grown up and quit trying to mold me into something I'm not."

He had his own opinion about that. But right now he didn't think she was in the mood to hear it. So he shifted the subject to something a little less controversial. At least to her. "Wanna tell me about the Proteans?" Stories about genetically engineered children had been in every respectable and nonrespectable paper since hundreds of billions of dollars had disappeared from the World Bank over a year ago. The techno heist had crashed the stock markets and shaken the financial stability of half the countries in the world.

She hesitated. "Look, Brady. I made a decision back there to trust you to hear information and not report it. But…"

"But now you're wondering if your trust goes that far."

"Actually, I'm pretty sure it does. Mainly because the Proteans have children now, many of them, anyway. And I don't think you'd hurt them. But still, I'd like to hear from your own lips that anything said on that path, anything I say now isn't going to show up in print."

There wasn't a reporter in the world who wouldn't kill for this story. While rumors and speculation had abounded about genetically engineered kids who'd grown into adults with almost superhuman powers being involved in the World Bank heist, no actual facts had been unearthed. Having those facts would give him the scoop of a lifetime. But… "Do you really think I'd run a story that would put you in danger? That would hurt *you?*"

She hesitated, a spark of something that looked like surprise in her eyes. But then her expression turned serious again. "The danger won't last forever. Once that sub's in the water…"

"Once the sub is in the water it's not a story anymore. So consider the sub off the table," he said a little impatiently. Did she really think he was some lowlife reporter that raced to the printer without giving thought to the havoc his piece could create? "As for the Proteans, I won't be writing about them, either. But not because of the kids. I won't be writing about them because you care about them. If they got hurt because of something you said and I wrote, you wouldn't blame me, you'd blame yourself. And I would never hurt you that way."

She gave him a warm smile and leaned against him. "You wouldn't hurt the kids that way, either. But thanks for thinking of me. On a day like today, it's much appreciated."

He gave her a hug, drinking in her softness, her warmth. "No problem. Now tell me about the Proteans. I might be willing to forgo writing about them, but I definitely want to hear about them."

She shrugged. "I'll be happy to tell you what I can, but it's not much. Just as they thought I should be kept out of the sub loop, my father thought I should be kept out of the Protean loop. I can tell you there were genetic engineering experiments in the sixties and seventies that included six kids. One of whom was my cousin Marcus."

"The guy they had checking on my background?"

She nodded. "He's Drew's brother, by the way."

"The pilot with the Rebelian spies?"

She nodded. "They were both in the navy. It's my guess Marcus has kept contact with the navy and that's why they had him checking your background."

"So Marcus is a Protean."

She nodded.

"Which means Drew is, too. Right?"

She shook her head. "Marcus is adopted. After Drew was born, my aunt and uncle had trouble conceiving, but they wanted another child. So they adopted a little boy."

He thought about the news stories he'd read. "So the adoption stories were true. How did that happen? I would think whoever created these kids would want to keep track of them."

"That story's a bit tricky. I have to go back to the beginning for it to make any sense. And I don't have all the pieces, so…" She ran her fingers through her hair, her expression thoughtful. "I might as well start with Henry Bloomfield. He was the genetic engineer behind the project's conception. And I think he was a good guy. I think all he wanted was to create bright, intelligent, healthy babies. But you know how that goes in the real world. Someone comes up with a way to improve mankind and someone else comes up with a way to use that knowledge against us."

He nodded.

"Well, Henry had good things in mind, but the scientists he was working with weren't so benevolent. They wanted to use the children's keen intelligence and physical abilities to create their own little seat of power. And apparently, they were dabbling in mind control with the children to achieve their ends. When Henry and Violet—Violet was the woman who carried the engineered embryos and who acted as a mother for the children—found out about the mind control and other scientists' plans they were incensed. But before they could do anything, Henry was killed.'' She grimaced.

"By the bad scientists?''

"It was ruled an accident at the time, but Violet was pretty sure they'd done it. And later when they drugged her and tried to steal the children, she knew she was right.''

His eyes went wide. "They drugged her?''

She nodded, disgust for the bad scientists and anger on Violet's behalf clear in her expression. "Once she managed to get herself and the kids out of that mess she realized she couldn't keep them anymore. She was afraid that as a group they'd be too easy to track. She decided the children would be safer if she dispersed them and thought adopting them out to different families was the best way to hide them. Luckily, a trusted friend of Henry's was able to help her get the children to safe families. Families who didn't know anything about the children's origins or powers.''

"But the children knew who they were, where they'd come from. How did she convince them to keep their identities secret?''

"She didn't have to. Remember that brainwashing I talked about?''

Surprise zinged through him. "I thought you said that was the bad guys.''

"Mostly it was. But Violet, obviously fearing the kids might give themselves away, had a man named

Leo Doppler brainwash them to erase their memories of their earlier childhoods. For years, most of them didn't remember anything of Violet and Henry and the house on the beach where they'd lived for the first part of their lives. Or the not-so-nice games the bad scientists had played with them.''

From the look on her face, he was pretty sure she wouldn't mind running into those people now. She'd like nothing better than to exact a little revenge for the Proteans. "That's an incredible story.''

She nodded. "It is, isn't it? And scary. To think of the extent some people will go for a little power.''

"Power's a mighty motivator. Just ask me. Every war zone I've ever been in has been generated by someone's thirst for power. And power mongers never care how many people pay the price for their thirst.'' He shook his head, thinking of all the misery he'd seen. But that was off the subject. "So, back to the story. Violet adopted the children out and Marcus ended up in the Evans family.''

She nodded. "And we're glad he did. He's a great guy.''

He smiled at her obvious affection for her cousin, her loyalty to family. "I'll bet he is. So if Violet was able to get them away from the bad guys—''

"The Coalition.''

He raised a brow in question.

"The Coalition. That's what the bad scientists eventually called themselves,'' she explained.

He cocked a brow. "That's a nice bit of melo-drama."

"What can I say? The fancy name made them feel self-important."

"So, if Violet got the kids away from the Coali-tion, how did they end up involved in the World Bank Heist?"

She grimaced. "Because she wasn't able to get all the children away. One child was left behind. And he was the one who engineered the heist. Strictly because the Coalition had kept him completely se-cluded and brainwashed, mind you. He didn't know what was right and what was wrong. I think he barely knew who he was." Her voice was thick with sym-pathy for the man as well as outrage at the people who kept him, bent him to their will.

He held up his hands. "Easy, I'm not accusing anyone. I'm just asking questions and listening."

"Sorry. I just get…"

"Passionate is the word you're looking for. You get passionate when you're talking about things that matter to you. And family matters to you. It's obvi-ous you consider the Proteans part of your family now."

Her brows snapped together. "Of course they're family. They're Marcus's brothers and sisters."

He smiled. What would it be like to have such passion, such care directed at him? His heart squeezed. It was a wasted thought. In order to create that type of bond a man had to stay in one place longer than a few weeks at a time. With his itchy feet, he wasn't capable of that. And he'd promised himself long ago that he wouldn't flit in and out of a woman's life, keeping her emotionally tied to him when he wouldn't be around enough to give her the love she needed on a daily basis.

He pushed the thought away. "Get back to our story. One of the children got left behind and he was the mastermind behind the heist."

She nodded. "If you remember, the World Bank was stunned after the heist. They'd been positive their computer security couldn't be breached. They'd said it would take a master genius to have gotten in. Violet knew right away that genius had to be her son. She immediately contacted Jake, the oldest of the Proteans. He didn't know who she was, of course. Not right away. But when she told him the story of his birth and the place they'd lived when he was younger, he knew the odd memories of the house by the beach and the people there hadn't been his imagination. They'd been real."

"Can you imagine your long-lost mother coming up to you and telling such a wild story?"

"No, thank God. But luckily the brainwashing wasn't totally thorough and Jake had enough memories to back up Violet's words. Once he realized what was going on, he set out to bring the kids back together. And to make sure the Coalition didn't get its hands on the scientific notes detailing the process Henry used to engineer the children."

He cocked a surprised brow. "They didn't already have the notes? Weren't they all working together?"

"They were working together, but apparently, Henry had had some misgivings about the other scientists. And since he was the brains behind the project, he kept his notes private. When things really started getting weird, he hid them, thank God, otherwise, the Coalition would have an army of little superhumans to do their bidding."

"Since you have a collection of the Proteans here helping at Evans Yachts, I take it Jake and Violet were successful."

A dark shadow crossed her face. "Jake was able to find all the Proteans, yes. And they found Henry's notes, too. Unfortunately, Violet didn't make it."

He sighed. "I'm sorry."

"Me, too. I would like to have met her."

He could see that she would have. "But the Coalition members have been rounded up, haven't they?"

"The main players, yes. But there were a lot of side players that are still out there. DeBruzkya for one."

"How does he figure in?"

"The FBI believes he was financially supporting the Coalition for a while."

"In hopes of using their abilities to further his cause?"

She nodded. "But they haven't been able to prove their connection."

"And now he's moved on to other things, like trying to get your brother's sub?"

"Apparently."

He shook his head. "Boy, what a story. Superheroes, mad scientists, grand schemes, conspiracy, murder and mayhem. It's got everything." And he was passing up the chance to be the one to expose it to the world.

He was either the biggest fool on earth.

Or he was in love.

No. He rejected the thought immediately. Rejected the bubble of excitement that filled his chest. Not love. Men like him didn't do love. Love took long-term commitment, something he wasn't capable of. And if he thought he was, all he had to do was remember the look on his mother's face every time his father left for one of his adventures. Remember her sadness. Remember the booze and pills she took to assuage that sadness. Remember what was really on the line if he tried to make a go of it with someone…and failed.

And he would surely fail. If he stayed in any place more than two weeks he got twitchy. Nope. He couldn't be in love. He knew better.

But lust?

He smiled, his gaze dropping to the low neckline of her swimsuit. She was wearing a bright blue one today that showed a little more cleavage than the white one. Yeah, lust he could indulge in. She had him wound tighter than a hangman's noose.

The other night she'd said they were getting closer. Maybe once they got this dive behind them and she quit worrying so much about the article, he could push her closer still. Sounded like a plan to him.

He smiled, watching the waves slide by beneath them. "So, how much farther do we have to go before we hit the reefs?"

Austin sat on the rail of the *Dancing Lady* as he prepared to tip backward into the ocean. He was anxious to get this dive done. Then, with any luck, he'd spend the rest of the afternoon in hedonistic bliss. Providing he found the right words to coax Laura into bed.

Not that he'd had much luck with his coaxing in the past. But he'd try harder this afternoon. For some reason it felt more...crucial. He wasn't sure why. Maybe because the article was almost done and the pictures he'd take today would bring him close to the end. Which meant he'd start getting itchy feet any day. And he somehow knew that if he left here without getting closer to Laura, without tasting her passion, her caring, even if it was only for a short time, he'd be losing something big. Something important.

But he couldn't think about what he'd planned for this afternoon, not dressed in a pair swimming trunks, not unless he wanted to embarrass them both. So he concentrated on the dive and on getting it behind them. Not that he'd let Laura know the dive was the last thing on which he wanted to waste even a minute of the day. He'd learned his lesson on that.

These reefs were important to her. So he'd pay attention. Even if it bored him to death.

Laura picked up his camera off the deck. "You ready to go in?"

Since his regulator was in his mouth, making talking impossible, he nodded.

"Okay, have at it. I'll hand you your camera once you're in. And don't forget to grab hold of your mask and regulator until you splash down."

Right. Securing his regulator and mask with one hand, he put his other hand behind his head to keep his tank from knocking him in the head. Then taking a deep breath from the tank, he rolled off the boat into the ocean. He hit the water upside down and simply relaxed until his air-filled BC brought him up to the surface. It only took a few seconds before he bobbed to the top.

"You okay?" Laura asked, peering down from the rail.

He gave the okay sign, swam to the side of the boat and reached up for his camera.

After she handed it to him, she sat up on the edge of the rail, tipped back into the ocean and splashed down beside him. A few seconds later she surfaced a few feet away and pulled the regulator from her mouth. "Ready?"

He nodded.

"Okay, down we go."

Holding tight to his camera, he released the air from his BC and sank slowly below the surface. The eerie silence enveloped him and he took a quick look around. No dark shadows lurking on the murky edges today. Good. He hoped it stayed that way. He didn't want Laura trying to prove again how exciting the ocean was. Once had been more than enough.

She caught his attention and pointed below them.

He looked down. The bottom wasn't far below today—maybe forty feet—and it was filled with Laura's precious reefs. He raised the camera and clicked off a few shots from a bird's eye view. He had to admit, it was colorful. Reds, browns, purples, blues. And there were fish darting everywhere. So many he couldn't begin to tell one species from another.

As they floated down, Laura wrote on a small magnetic slate he'd seen her attaching to her BC earlier. When they made it to the reefs she pointed to a specific piece of coral and turned the slate toward him.

"Fan coral" was written on the white surface.

He nodded. The slate would undoubtedly come in handy, but he was familiar with fan coral from the one snorkeling trip he'd been on. After all, its delicate, lacy form was very distinct.

She swam away, her movements too deliberate for her to be just meandering along the reef. She obviously had a destination in mind. He followed until she came to a stop and pointed to another piece of coral he recognized. Brain coral, so named because it looked like…well, a brain. But this specimen was huge, as big as a small boulder. He clicked off several pictures.

She scrawled on the magnetic slate and turned it toward him.

"Brain coral."

He nodded.

She erased the words, scribbled again and turned the slate for his perusal.

"This coral was born right after the Ice Age."

The Ice Age? Wow. That would make it…ten *thousand* years old. Give or take a thousand or two.

She crooked her finger again and swam to the other side of the big coral. When he joined her, she pointed to a small white circle on the rounded surface, a place no bigger than a dime. The spot was some type of disease. He couldn't remember which one. She'd shown him dozens in the past few days. She scribbled on the slate again and turned it to him.

It'll be dead in a year.

Shock ripped through him. A year? It had lived through thousands of years, had seen the ocean grow and change in countless ways, and now this disease would kill it in a year?

For the first time he understood some of Laura's frustration. Some of the immediacy she felt about saving these reefs. To think that something that had been around since the time of mammoths, for crying out loud, was still living today… It was amazing.

And sad to think that its demise was imminent. He was lucky he'd been on this dive, that he'd been able to see it before it disappeared.

He would have stayed for a while and just admired it, but Laura was swimming off again, her pace ambitious. He swam after her, admiring her sexy legs as they kicked gently through the water, totally appreciating the perfect view he had of her butt. He thought about clicking off a few pictures. But he'd promised to behave himself so he kept his camera angled at the reefs.

As they swam along, Laura pointed out different types of coral and the different species of fish, naming many of them on her slate. Her enthusiasm made him want to smile, but every time he did, his mask flooded with briny seawater, stinging his eyes and nose, and he had to clear it, so he resisted the temptation. But it was hard. She was so passionate about it all. The coral, the fish, the anemones.

Unfortunately, he wasn't going to remember half the species he'd taken pictures of. The names and images came at him too fast and furiously here where the reefs were packed with different kinds of corals and hundreds of types of fish. And her pace was downright relentless. He'd have to remind her when they got to the surface that they were supposed to be swimming at a relaxed pace, saving their oxygen.

Yeah, Austin Brady giving scuba lessons to Laura Evans. She'd love that. He chuckled, the muffled sound reverberating through the water.

Laura looked over at him.

He just shrugged, pointing to a funny-looking fish to make her think that was what he was laughing at. But he was enjoying the moment. Enjoying the passion of the woman next to him. Enjoying—to his amazement—the diversity of the species around him. The reefs he'd explored snorkeling had been nothing like these. There'd been only a few species of fish and coral there. And, of course, Laura hadn't been on that trip, sharing her enthusiasm for the underwater world.

As they moved down the reef, things finally slowed a little. The reefs got sparser, as did the fish population. And since she'd already shown him ninety-nine percent of the species living here, she was writing on her slate less. They swam side by side, a pastime he enjoyed far more than he would have imagined.

Yeah, he could spend a lot of time down here— with Laura at his side, of course. There was a peacefulness he'd never felt before. Amazing. But there it was. He slowed his kicking a little more and dropped back so that Laura was in front of him. As much as he was enjoying the fish and other scenery, there was nothing as interesting or beautiful as Laura. He swam behind her, admiring the graceful movement of her legs, the tanned smoothness of her skin, the curvy temptation of her backside.

Suddenly she stopped and turned to him, waving one hand expansively in front of her.

He snapped his attention back to his purpose for being down here. He'd been so busy watching her, he hadn't noticed the drastic change in the ocean. And there had certainly been one. There were no colors here. Just the white sand, a little lumpier here than it had been where they'd first dropped into the water, and the occasional aquatic plant.

Laura sifted through the white bottom and held up a piece of something.

He swam closer to get a better look. Surprise washed over him. She was holding the bleached-out skeleton of a piece of coral. He looked around him again. The white skeletons were everywhere. That was what made the sand lumpy. Dead coral.

She scribbled on her slate and turned it to him.

"Look around you. How many fish do you see?"

He did a full three-sixty, peering deeply into the murky edges.

There were almost no fish.

He looked back to her, his surprise turning to shock, their gazes meeting through their masks.

Seeing his surprise, she nodded, wrote on the slate again and turned it to him.

"Do you know how many people depend on fish as their main food source?"

Okay, that was serious. He looked around again, snapping several pictures. The fish he saw around him wouldn't feed a single family. Scary. It was one thing to hear that the world's fish supplies were dwindling, to hear that fishermen's catches were declining by the month. But to see it firsthand was a shocking eye-opener. He looked over to Laura.

She held her thumb up, indicating it was time to return to the surface.

He trailed her up to the boat that had followed them as they swam down the reef. After handing their fins and BCs up to Andre, they climbed on board. Water pouring off him, Austin pulled his mask off. "Okay, you've convinced me. Those reefs are important. Ecologically and aesthetically. What on earth happened down there?"

She shot him a droll look. "You know what happened down there. You *have* been paying attention at the lab, haven't you?"

"Yeah." He sat down, her words of the past days echoing through his head. Pesticides, African dust, waste.

"You tired?"

He looked up, smiling. "Let's just say I feel like I've had a workout."

"I pushed us a little because I wanted you to see both the brain coral and the dead part of the reef."

"*That* was cool. Ten thousand years old? Really?"

She nodded. "You bet. I wanted you to see that piece because there are so few ancient corals left. I've seen footage of people diving these reefs in the sixties. You wouldn't believe the difference. Remember the pillar corals I showed you?"

"The ones that looked like little termite hills, but with rounded tops? Reddish brown about six inches to a couple feet tall? Sometimes they branch out like deformed cactus?''

"That would be them. In the sixties there were forests of them. And they weren't a couple feet high, they were twenty-five feet tall. And bigger around than a man. Can you imagine?''

He shook his head. "It must have been amazing.''

She looked out to sea, her expression wistful. "Yeah, I wish I could have seen them.''

"But you've been diving a long time, right? Were they all gone by the time you started diving?''

"The really big ones were gone. They were cut down to make it easier for boats to get through and to use in gardens and jewelry. But there were a lot more big corals when I was younger than there are now. I'm glad I got to see those.''

"I'm glad I got to see that brain coral. Amazing.''

She grabbed a towel, wrapped it around herself and then handed him one. "Hey, be glad you saw the reefs at all. If we don't find a way to turn things around, in ten more years they won't exist anymore.''

He stared out to sea, a sense of loss stealing through him. Loss and alarm. "I think the scariest thing I saw down there was the lack of fish.''

She nodded. "There are a lot of reasons for that, of course, overfishing being one. But a big part of it is the disappearance of the reef. Fish need the ecosystem to live and without it...''

"No fish.''

"You got it. But just as important as the loss of fish and the food source they provide is the loss of opportunity. The reefs are the most diverse ecosystem on earth. Even more diverse than the rain forest. The potential for future products, future medicines is immense. And we're going to lose the system before we've had a chance to really explore it."

His gaze locked on to hers. "We'll write a great article. I know it's not much but it's the one thing I can do. Caleb's given us six pages to make a statement. I'll call tomorrow and push for eight."

A smile of pure joy turned her lips and she sat next to him, throwing her arms around him for a big hug. "You have no idea how much I wanted to hear those words." She gave him a kiss on the cheek. "Thank you."

Heat poured through him, and his hopes for the afternoon climbed a notch. "No problem." Hell, if that was all it took for her to touch him, he'd have said those words a long time ago.

She pulled her arms from around him, but she stayed sitting next to him, their chilled bodies creating welcome warmth where their hips and shoulders touched. "I'm glad you finally understand. Now, if my folks would read the article, maybe they'd finally understand I'm not wasting my life out here."

"Come on, Laura. I don't think your parents think you're wasting your life."

"Trust me, that's exactly what they think." Her

lips pressed together in irritation. "They think I'm out here playing in the waves, and if they just wait long enough, I'll come to my senses and go to work at Evans Yachts."

He shook his head. "Look, I know there's friction between you and your parents. I can understand your frustration with them about the sub plans and the other things they've kept from you. No one likes to be kept out of the loop. Although I have to point out that I don't think they kept those things from you to hurt you. I do think your dad was trying to protect you."

She snapped her gaze to his. "You can't be serious. You heard him say he wasn't sure that was his only motivation. That he thought maybe he was trying to pressure me into coming to work at Evans Yachts."

"Yeah, I heard. But you know what? Having your dad want you to work at the family business is hardly a cardinal sin. It means he cares about you. It means that maybe your parents and your brothers would like to see a little more of you. Those aren't bad things. Take it from me. My father never gave a good damn where I was or what I was doing, and my mother was so wrapped up in her grief over my father's constant absence that she didn't care, either. Having someone interested in you and your welfare is not a bad thing. It's a good thing. A very good thing."

She looked at him in outrage. "Are you on their side?"

Oh boy, he should shut up. He was just ticking her off, which was the last thing he wanted to do. But he wasn't going to back down on this. This was important. "No, believe it or not, I'm on your side. Which does not necessarily mean buying into your poor-me routine. I think you have some legitimate reasons for being upset with your parents. But I also think you could try a little harder to understand where they're coming from."

She pushed off the bench. "You don't get it, Brady. I'm not saying they don't love me. I'm saying they don't respect me. Or the profession I've chosen." With a shake of her head, she strode off.

He sighed, watching her move away from him across the deck. Yep, he could kiss this afternoon's plans goodbye.

Eleven

Halfway back to the dock, Austin sat on deck and watched Laura pull the dive gear apart and put it away. Normally he would have helped with the chore, but he didn't think she'd appreciate his help at the moment. Her movements were getting smoother, her natural gracefulness returning as her pique cooled. But beyond an occasional surreptitious peek, she still wasn't looking at him. Or making any effort to talk with him.

Her cold shoulder was making for a dull trip back to shore, but he wasn't taking his words back. He couldn't remember how many nights he'd lain awake as a boy wishing he had a real family. Wishing his family would stay together for more than the occasional day or two every three or four months. Wishing that when his family was together, they'd do things together.

Not big things like going to Disney or Yosemite. That would have been too much to ask for. But he had wished they'd do some of the smaller things most families seemed to do. Things like having dinner together or watching TV together. Anything that would have shown him his parents even knew he was on the planet.

Laura had that. Her parents obviously loved her deeply. And he knew Laura loved them. He also knew how important family was to her. This little fight they were having over where she worked was ridiculous, on both their parts. And he was damned well not going to pretend it wasn't. He'd watched too many families torn apart by war or other real tragedies to watch a family who loved each other squabble over petty problems. Love was too precious a commodity for that kind of nonsense.

In the distance, a bell clanged.

He straightened, glancing around for the source of the sound. A small motorboat bobbed in the distance, heading their way. The boat was too far away to make out much about it, but he could see one of the three men on board was waving his arms. He looked back to Laura.

She was watching the boat, too, her hands stilling as she took in the scene.

"What do you think that's about?" he asked.

She shook her head, her brows pulled low in concern. "I don't know, but waving your arms like that usually means you're in trouble." She set down the fins she'd been putting in her dive bag and strode toward the back of the cabin so she could see the helm. "Hey, Ted, did you see that boat?"

He nodded. "Should we heave to?"

"Yeah. Maybe we can help."

Ted hollered at Andre, and the sails were adjusted. The *Dancing Lady* slowed and went quiet in the water.

Austin joined Laura at the rail and watched the smaller boat's approach. "Whatever their problem is, it's not their motor. It's running fine," he said.

She nodded, her mood still a bit chilly. "Yep. I see that."

He looked heavenward. "Come on, Laura. You're not going to hold a grudge all afternoon, are you?"

She shot him a sideways glance. "Give me one reason I shouldn't."

He gave her his most winning smile. "Because I'm a handsome, charming man, full of fun and hard to resist?"

She managed to hold on to her pique for a full three seconds before she broke down and laughed, shaking her head. "What you are is the most arrogant man I know."

"Yeah, well, that, too. But still endearing, right?"

She laughed again, pointing out to sea. "Let's pay attention to the boat in trouble, shall we? You can stroke your ego later."

He looked back out to the approaching boat. "So what do you think their problem is?"

"I don't know. But you're right, it's definitely not their motor. They're coming at us like gangbusters. They might be low on fuel. Could be they're new to the ocean, got excited by the open water and ended up farther out than they thought."

He smiled. "How embarrassing."

She laughed with him. "No kidding."

He watched the boat get closer and closer. "For people low on fuel, they're sure not sparing any to get to us. They're running full out. Maybe they're just lost."

"If they don't know how to read a compass, I suppose. But whatever their problem, it has to be something goofy like that. No one looks hurt."

No, they didn't. The three men were standing in the boat upright, looking plenty healthy. He suddenly remembered the conversation about subs and spies. A frisson of unease ran through him. "Is it common for people to run out of gas or get lost out here?"

She shrugged. "It doesn't happen often. But I've come across it before."

That answer didn't make him feel a whole lot better. "How many times? Once? Twice? Fifteen times?"

She looked over at him. "Why?"

"I don't know. I just suddenly have a bad feeling."

Her brows pulled together in question. "A bad feeling? About the boat?"

"Look, I know this sounds paranoid, but with all the things you've mentioned going on in your family lately, boats blowing up, attempted kidnappings, people hacking into computers, DeBruzkya, maybe we should approach this with a little more caution than normal."

She rolled her eyes. "It's not *that* unusual for someone to run into trouble on the open sea and hail help."

"You sure? When was the last time someone approached your boat out here?"

"I don't know, a few years ago, I think. A family had gone fishing and their motor conked out. Ted and I found them floating along in the waves."

"You found them," he pointed out. "They didn't find you."

"Well, people have approached the boat I was in once or twice."

Urgency pushed at him as the boat drew ever closer. "Once or twice," he stressed. "Not much for someone who spends as much time on the ocean as you do."

"True, but—"

"Listen, I've walked into more than one ambush while reporting on wars in Third World countries. I've learned to be cautious. That's all I'm asking you to do here. Be careful. Let's make sure who these guys are before we let them get too close or, for crying out loud, before we invite them on board."

She rolled her eyes. "Fine."

It wasn't the enthusiastic response he'd hoped for, but he'd take it. Especially since the motorboat was almost upon them.

The smaller craft slowed its engines, the loud roar turning into a guttural chugging.

Austin studied the men in the small boat. The

driver waved and smiled eagerly—too eagerly in Austin's opinion. But he could see both the man's hands so Austin dismissed him as a threat. An immediate one, anyway.

He moved his focus to the two men flanking the driver. The man who'd been waving his arms to catch their attention earlier was quiet now and he had his right hand tucked behind him. The hairs on the back of Austin's neck stood up, and he quickly looked to the third man in the boat. His right arm was tucked behind his back, too.

Not good.

Austin pitched his voice loud enough for Laura to hear over the thrum of the smaller craft's motor, but not loud enough for their visitors' ears. "Notice how both men behind the driver are holding their right arms behind them?"

She shot him a quizzical glance. "Yeah. So?"

"Call it paranoia, but they could be hiding weapons."

To his great satisfaction, it wasn't a you're-crazy look that crossed her face this time. It was one of concern. She glanced back to the smaller craft. "All right, now you have me worried." A nervous little laugh slipped from her lips. "When this turns out to be nothing, I'm going to make you feel like such an idiot."

"Not a problem. I can eat crow with the best of them."

A tight smile on her lips, she held her hands up,

indicating the motorboat should stop where it was. "That's close enough, guys," she hollered. "We don't need the waves crashing us together."

"Good. A legitimate reason to keep them from getting too close."

"Hey, you want caution, you get caution."

And he was glad of it. Now that they were closer he could see two men were smiling, but the third had a dour, businesslike expression—one Austin had seen on more than one soldier bent on getting the job done. And neither of the men with their arms behind their backs, despite the rocking of the boat, had let those arms slip for even a moment from their hidden position.

Austin leaned on the rail and raised his voice. "What's up, gentlemen? Trouble on board?"

The driver smiled wider, holding up a map. "We're looking for a specific fishing place and couldn't find it. We thought you might know where it is."

Wearing khaki dockers and T-shirts, the boaters certainly looked like they could be out for an afternoon of fishing.

"If they think I'm going to help them catch my fish, they're dreaming," Laura muttered.

He smiled. Despite the tension vibrating around them, she was still thinking about her fish. "If they're legit, you can send them in the wrong direction. In the meantime—" He tipped his head toward the map and raised his voice. "What spot are you looking for?"

"We're looking for Taninger's reef."

"Oh yeah, I'm going to send them—" She gasped. "Brady, they don't have any fishing gear."

His gaze flew over the boat. *Son of a bitch.* She was right. They might be dressed like weekend fishermen, but there wasn't a pole in sight.

He turned to her as if they were discussing the fishing spot. "Okay, keep cool. Keep smiling. Let's see if we can send them on their way." He turned back to the poleless fishermen and shrugged his shoulders. "Sorry, gentlemen, we aren't familiar with your spot. Good luck finding it, though." He turned toward the helm. "Let's continue on, Ted. Andre, sails up."

He'd barely gotten the words out when the rifles appeared from behind the strangers' backs. "We're sorry," the driver said, his smile never slipping. "That won't be possible. We need to detain Miss Evans for a bit. General DeBruzkya would like to speak with her."

Austin's stomach turned, fear pouring through him as he remembered the savage tales Rebelians told of DeBruzkya's handling of enemies. Hell, the megalomaniac didn't handle his own citizens any better. The thought of Laura in his hands...

No way in hell he was letting that happen. He kept his eyes locked on the automatic rifles pointed their way. "Laura, DeBruzkya isn't the kind of man to ask politely for information. Nor is he the type of man to release a hostage if his only intention is to hold you for ransom until your brother hands over the information he wants.''

Fear shone in her eyes, but she kept her chin up. ''I know his reputation,'' she said. ''I'm not turning over our men or this boat to that bastard. Or myself, for that matter.''

''Run?''

''Absolutely.''

Without another word, he grabbed Laura and dived for the deck. ''Get us out of here, Ted. Andre, get those sails up.'' Automatic gunfire exploded around them. Small holes appeared in the boat's side.

''Quick, get on the other side of the cabin.'' He tried to push Laura in that direction.

But she just turned back toward the helm. ''Ted, stick the thing on autopilot and get out of there. Andre, get down. I'll get the sails.''

''The hell you will.'' Austin grabbed her when she tried to stand, pulling her back down.

Luckily Andre had the sail up before they could argue over it any longer. He lashed it tight and sprinted for the far side of the cabin.

''Get down,'' Austin hollered after the young man as more shots rang over their heads.

The kid dived to the deck and disappeared behind the cabin faster than a sidewinder flying across the desert.

Austin pushed Laura in the same direction. "Get over there."

She looked back toward the helm. "Ted?"

"I'm coming, Laura. *Go.*"

With bullets flying over their heads, they crawled to the other side of the cabin. They'd barely joined Andre when Ted came flying around the corner from the opposite direction. "Autopilot's on."

Laura went limp with relief. "Good. Now what?"

What, indeed? The Rebelian thugs were still firing at the side of the *Dancing Lady*, obviously unaware their quarry had crawled to the other side of the vessel and hidden behind the cabin. But they'd figure it out before long. Unless… Austin looked at Ted. "What are our chances of outrunning them?"

The captain shook his head. "Not going to happen. They have a light little souped-up motorboat. We're twice as big, twice as heavy—and we're on sails."

"What if we use the motor?"

Again he shook his head. "It's just an auxiliary motor, nothing fancy. It's designed to get the boat to port or out of a becalmed area if the wind dies, nothing more."

Dammit. "So our only real game plan is to avoid getting shot before we hit shore?"

Ted nodded. "That's about it."

"Great."

Another round of bullets sprayed the boat.

"Everybody below," Austin said. "The bullets

have to go through two walls to get us here, but down below they have to go through water and then the hull to reach us. That has to be our best bet. Go, go, go.''

They all scrambled for the stairs, Austin making sure Laura went first, then Andre and Ted. He followed. He was just ducking into the cabin at the top of the stairs when a loud thump sounded and the *Dancing Lady* shuddered.

Laura whipped her head around, her eyes meeting his. ''They're trying to board. That attempt failed. They just bounced off or we'd be hearing continual bumping. But if they keep trying, they'll probably get it right.''

Damn. He looked to Ted. ''Any weapons on board?''

''Not unless you count the two fire axes.''

''That's what I like—a fair fight. Automatic rifles against axes. Damn, I feel like a peasant in the French Revolution. Where are the axes?''

Laura nodded her head toward the stairs. ''One's hanging on the wall just outside the companionway door there. The other one's down here.''

''I'll get the one up here. Ted, you get the other.'' He looked to Andre. ''Can you raise the coast guard on the radio?''

''Yeah, but don't hold your breath. They're probably hours away.''

''Call anyway.''

Austin scrambled out of the companionway,

grabbed the ax from its place on the wall and, staying low, moved to the side of the cabin. Peeking around the corner, he looked for any boarders.

None.

But another thump against the hull confirmed they were still trying.

A hand landed on his shoulder.

He jumped.

"Are they on board?" Laura whispered in his ear.

"Laura, you scared me to death. I thought you were one of the Rebelians. And what the *hell* are you doing up here? Get below."

"No way. If you're fighting, I'm fighting."

Fear exploded in his chest at the mere thought of her facing men as ruthless as DeBruzkya's henchmen. But if he pulled the macho-man thing, it would just tick her off. Maybe a reality check would get him further. He gave her a droll look. "Had a lot of experience with hand-to-hand combat, have you?"

Scowling, she raised that stubborn chin. "Probably as much as a journalist."

"If you'll think about where I tend to do my reporting from, you'll realize that probably isn't so. I've had to fight my way out of more than one Third World hellhole."

"All right, you might have a point. But I'm still not going anywhere."

"Laura—"

"Andre got through to the guard," Ted said, crawling out of the companionway, the ax held firmly in his hands. "They're an hour out. Said they'd have the cops waiting at the shore."

"Great. All we have to do is make it that far."

"So it would seem." The captain looked to Laura. "Andre's radioing your folks right now. He didn't want the cops screaming into their driveway to be their first hint of trouble."

She nodded. "Thanks, Ted."

"No problem." The wiry captain motioned toward the far side of the boat. "Who do you think our friends are?"

Austin and Laura exchanged a glance but neither said anything. If Russ Evans hadn't told his daughter what was going on with the sub, Austin was pretty sure he wouldn't want an employee knowing about it. Luckily, he'd been too far back to hear the conversation going on between the *Dancing Lady* and the smaller craft. He hadn't heard DeBruzkya's name. But he didn't have a clue what explanation to offer in place of the truth.

"Pirates?" Ted asked.

Austin grabbed on to the guess. "Maybe."

"Makes sense if they're after Laura. She'd be the one to ransom."

Austin nodded. "Makes sense. But for now, let's worry about getting rid of them. We can speculate on who they are later." His attention caught on the air tanks strapped to the boat's side. "Holy saving light."

Laura's gaze narrowed on him. "What?"

He tipped his head toward the tanks. "Those are going to be much better weapons than the axes."

She glanced at the tanks with a questioning look. But then she got it. A wicked smile turned her lips. "Pressurized air. We knock those tops off, they're going to fly like missiles."

He smiled back. "Lethal missiles."

Ted's expression brightened as he, too, realized the power of the usually benign tanks. "We can use the axes to knock the tops off."

Austin nodded just as another thump came from the side of the boat. And then another. "Let's get on it before our friends figure out the boarding thing. What's the construction of this boat like, Ted? If we use the deck as a launching pad, which means the tanks would have to go through the railing over there, are we going to sink this sucker?"

"The closer to the top of the rail they hit, the safer we're going to be. Shooting over the rail entirely would be the best."

Austin shook his head. "That's going to be too high to do us any good. The tank will sail right over our pirates' heads." He looked around. "Is there anything on board we can drag over to set the tanks on? Something that would give us a little more height?"

"I've got a research chest." Ducking, Laura ran back toward the helm.

He made a grab for her just as she left the protection of the cabin. And missed.

Bullets started firing.

He dived after her, knocking her to the deck. "Stay down, dammit. And if you won't go downstairs, stay behind the cabin. I'll get the chest." He crawled over to the chest and dragged it back with him. Once he was behind the cabin, he got up and pushed the chest out the other side, just beyond the cabin's walls, where they could get a tank up on it without exposing themselves.

Once he had it set, he peeked around the corner, conscious of the constant thumping coming from the other side of the boat. "They've got grappling hooks and ropes on the rail. Let's get a tank up here *fast.*"

Luckily there were about six tanks stored behind the protection of the cabin. Ted grabbed one from the wall and, keeping his body hidden behind the cabin as much as possible, set the tank out on the chest.

"Everybody back," Austin ordered. "We don't actually have any idea where this damn thing's going."

To his great relief no one argued. They all fell behind him. He raised the ax and brought it down hard on the metal coupling that capped off the top of the pressurized tank. The top popped off. The loud hissing of rapidly escaping air filled the deck as the tank wavered and then flew across the boat, crashing through the top railing. The boat rocked beneath their feet, the sound of shattering wood ringing in their ears.

Surprised, angry voices sounded on the other side of the boat. Followed by another round of bullets.

"Guess they didn't like that." Austin smiled coldly, peeking around the walls. "Damn. We have a *big* hole in the railing, Ted. What do you think?"

Ted glanced around the cabin. "The hole's wide, but it doesn't look like it goes down far. I don't think it reaches the deck. As long as the ocean stays quiet, we'll be fine."

"Good, because it sounds like our friends are determined to board." The motorboat still banged relentlessly against their hull. Unfortunately, their makeshift missile had missed the railing where the grappling hooks were attached. "Everyone back. We're firing again. Ted, get another tank up."

Ted quickly lifted another tank onto the chest.

Austin swung the ax.

The tank screamed off the chest. Another loud crash and then the sound of panicked voices.

Smiling, Austin hollered into the din. "We've got more where those came from, boys. Come on up."

There was a moment of silence. A round of shots. Then the sound of the small craft's engine revved. And receded.

Austin looked around the corner again. "They're pulling back."

"Regrouping or leaving?" Laura leaned around him, trying to get her own peek.

He pushed her back. "Stay back. They might be pulling away, but they still have their rifles."

She gave him a you're-spoiling-my-fun look, but she leaned back against the wall. "Sounds like they're falling behind us."

They all looked aft. Sure enough, the boat was coming in behind them, although not too close.

"Quick, everyone to the front of the cabin."

They all raced to the front, once again out of sight of the shooters.

Austin peeked around the corner at the Rebelians again. "They're not crowding us. They're staying back a bit. If we fire a tank off the chest, by the time it crashes through the railing, it might not have enough momentum to reach them. But if we fire one off of the roof..."

Ted smiled. "Gotcha." He snatched another tank from the wall, staying low to avoid the fresh round of shots. Then he reached up and set the tank on the edge of the cabin's roof, a few feet above their heads. "Fire away."

Austin swung the ax over his head.

The tank flew off the cabin.

Austin peeked out in time to see one of the men in the boat duck to keep the tank from taking off his head. There was another animated exchange between the bad guys and then the boat veered off, heading back out to sea.

Austin turned to the others. "They're leaving."

There was a collective sigh of relief as they all sank to the deck, the cabin at their backs, their legs stretched out in front of them.

Laura looked over at him, her eyes shining. "Well, that was…" A slow smile curved her lips. "Exciting. I'm beginning to see what it is you like about flying bullets and imminent danger."

Hell, there hadn't been an exciting thing about it. He'd felt nothing but the same bone-chilling fear he'd felt when Laura had snuggled up next to that damned shark.

And the fact that he'd found the battle frightening instead of exciting was as unsettling as the battle itself had been. In the past, the more dangerous the situation, the more he liked it. Even when there were other people he knew and liked involved in the situation, he still enjoyed the thrill. But with Laura it was different.

Way different.

And it was a difference he wasn't sure he wanted to examine too closely. He didn't want to think that Laura Evans was becoming too important to him. Didn't want to think that when he left, her image would haunt him. Didn't want to think that he'd hunger for her sweet, caring nature. Because the lonely nights that still caught up with him now and then were already dark enough. Long enough. He didn't need them to be any darker. Any longer.

Any lonelier.

Twelve

Laura stood next to the rail with Brady, watching the shoreline draw closer. She could see her family huddled on the dock waiting for them. The police were there, too, waiting for their arrival, their four uniformed figures standing off to the side with Raimes, her father's chief of security.

She looked to Brady. "We'll have to make sure we don't mention the sub when we're talking to the cops."

He nodded. "Don't worry. I won't let anything slip. I assume we're going to play dumb, like we did with Ted."

She nodded. "We'll stick to the facts. Three men in a boat came up and tried to take me. Let them draw their own conclusions." She looked back to the dock. Back to her family. They weren't close enough to see their expressions, but she couldn't guess what they were feeling. Her father had his arm protectively around her mother. Her brothers were pacing from one end of the dock to the other, their strides long and agitated.

She sighed, the events of the day closing in on her like dark shadows. She wanted to get home to her little house. She'd never thought of it as a safe haven before, but she did now. Unfortunately, she had a big scene to get through first.

Brady looked over to her. "You okay?"

"Yeah, I guess."

His lips twisted knowingly. "The reality of what just happened catching up with you?"

Scenes of the automatic rifles coming from behind the men's backs kept playing over and over in her mind. The driver's voice saying they needed to "detain" her echoed endlessly in her head. "Earlier I thought it was exciting. But now…"

Now her imagination kept putting different endings on the day's events. One of the bullets going through her body. The Rebelians capturing her and taking her back to DeBruzkya. The tanks exploding when they struck the tops off with the ax. She shivered at the thought.

Brady pulled her close, rubbing the goose bumps from her arms. "Now you're thinking about all the things that could have gone wrong. All the different endings the fight could have had." He shook his head. "Don't go there. Take a deep breath, shove the thoughts away and concentrate on this moment. Concentrate on the fact that no one was hurt."

She tried to do as he said, tried to force her mind to let the images go. But… "It would be a lot easier if I didn't feel so…"

He smiled. "Tired and edgy?"

"Yeah. How'd you know?"

"The end of an adrenaline jag. It'll wear off in a few hours. Then you'll really crash."

If anyone knew about adrenaline jags she would imagine it would be an adrenaline junkie. "As long as I hold up long enough to get through the scene waiting on the dock, I guess it doesn't matter."

He looked toward her family, his expression turning wary. "Laura, look, at the risk of offending you again, I'm going to throw a little warning in here. The downside of an adrenaline jag is *not* the time to get into old arguments. When we hit the dock, stay cool. Answer the cops' questions, let your family know you're all right and get out of there. Tomorrow is soon enough for arguments. You start one today, and you're likely to say something you'll regret."

She rubbed at the dull ache starting in her temples. "You're probably right. Besides, I just want to get home."

He gave her shoulders another squeeze. "Good."

As they approached the dock, Andre raced from one end of the boat to the other, tossing the mooring lines to Holt and Seth. They'd barely tied off the boat when her mom and dad boarded the *Dancing Lady,* concern written all over their faces.

Laura held out her hands. "We're fine, you guys. Nobody was hurt. Well, except for the boat." She waved a hand toward the gaping hole in the rail.

Her mother enclosed her in her arms, hanging on tight. "You sure you're okay?"

Laura squeezed back. "Fine, Mom. Really." She

soaked up the comfort her mother offered, then pulled out of her arms.

Her dad was looking at the giant hole in the rail, then sweeping the boat for additional damage. "What the hell did they hit you with?"

"Actually, that's from us hitting them." She waved a hand toward what was left of the tanks still hanging from the wall. "We used the air tanks as missiles."

Surprise crossed her father's face. "Good thinking."

"Very good thinking." The deep, gravelly voice belonged to Raimes, who had stepped up beside them. "I'm going to bring Ted and Andre down now. That'll keep the cops busy for a bit. You'll probably have about five minutes before they swarm on board."

Her father nodded.

Raimes strode away to gather the two crewmen.

Laura looked to her father. "Five minutes to get our story straight, huh? Don't worry, Brady and I have discussed the fact we won't be mentioning the sub. Or the real reason the men were after me. And you don't have to worry about Ted or Andre, either. They think the men were pirates, looking to ransom me."

Her father's gaze narrowed on her. "So the attackers *were* after you?"

"They said they wanted to 'detain' me. For DeBruzkya"

"Oh God, they probably wanted to use you for leverage, claiming they'd return you once we gave them the sub's plans." He closed his eyes briefly, then opened them, their brown depths locking on her with intensity. "But you're okay?"

Let it go. *Let it go.* But she just…couldn't. "Yeah, I'm fine, Dad. No thanks to you. If I hadn't happened along and heard that conversation earlier, I'd be in DeBruzkya's hands by now."

Next to her, Brady shot her a warning look. "Laura."

She tossed her hands. "I can't do it. I can't pretend everything is hunky-dory when we might have all ended up dead." She looked back to her father. "Dead, Dad. Because you thought you could blackmail me into going to work for Evans Yachts."

Her father reeled back as if she'd slapped him. But his surprise didn't last long. A red flush climbed up his neck. "I kept the information about the sub and spies from you because I wanted you *safe.* And if you'd quit playing around in the damned water and come to work where you belong I wouldn't *have* to blackmail you." He kept his voice low, making sure it didn't carry to the cops, but his anger wasn't any less potent because of it.

Laura leaned toward him, her own anger spiraling out of control. "So what are you saying? That you'd rather I end up *dead* than work at a job other than Evans Yachts?"

"All right, that's it." Austin stepped between

Laura and her dad. His gaze narrowed on her. "I thought we decided you weren't going to get into old arguments right now."

"I can change my mind, Brady."

He shook his head. "Not today you can't. I'm not going to let you. And while you're sulking about that fact, you should consider that while your dad is no doubt capable of applying pressure in any number of ways to get you to work at Evans Yachts, I don't believe for a moment he'd want you dead instead of working somewhere else. And neither do you," he finished pointedly.

She opened her mouth to disagree, but the words died on her tongue. Looking away, she ran a shaky hand through her hair. "You're right. But that doesn't mean—"

He slashed his hand through the air. "Not today, Laura."

She drew a steadying breath. He was right, her emotions were too raw. "Fine."

"Fine." He turned to her father. "And while I should leave it at that and let you two hash it out later, I just can't force myself do that. This family has a great thing going for it. You love one another, care for one another, but right now you're about to blow all that over something so trivial, you should both be ashamed. Your daughter *has* a career, Russ."

Her father drew his shoulders back and shot Brady a hard glare. "I'm well aware of that. And I'm sure you're aware this is none of your business."

Brady returned a cold smile. "Absolutely. But I'm sticking my nose in it, anyway. As I was saying, your daughter has a career." He held his hands up. "I know, you think it's a juvenile, frivolous waste of her time. I know when I took this assignment I thought Caleb was sending me on some fluff piece. A belief I pretty much held on to until this afternoon."

Laura gasped at the admission, irritation sliding through her.

Brady said quickly, "I don't think that anymore." Then he turned back to her dad. "Not anymore. After going down with Laura today, actually seeing the reefs she's trying to save, I understand how important that ecosystem is. How devastated it is. And how much work she's putting into saving it. Have you ever put on the gear and gone down with your daughter, Russ?"

"No, I haven't." Her father's voice was as stiff as a drawn sail.

"Well, you need to. You need to see and compare the healthy, thriving reefs near the end of the keys and the dead zone they become as you get closer to the tip of Florida. You need to see, firsthand, the way the fish population practically disappears. The world's population is getting bigger, not smaller. The world needs more food to feed its people, not less. Laura's trying to figure out a way to make that happen. That's an important job, Russ. Damned important. Far more important than helping to design a few fancy yachts. Now, I'm heading down to talk to the police. Anyone else coming?''

He strode away, leaving her staring, amazed, at his back.

An hour and a half later, Laura sat in her car—in the passenger's seat—waiting for Brady. She had the door open and was sitting with her feet hanging out, trying not to suffocate before he got there. The police interviews had gone on and on and on. But the police had finally asked every question they could think of a hundred times over and decided to head back to the station to finish their reports. The last squad car was pulling out of her parents' driveway now. Thank God.

She wanted this mess behind her. She didn't want to think about pirates or spies or bullets or air tanks. She wanted to think about what Brady had said earlier about her reefs—and her job.

That's an important job, Russ.

Far more important than helping to design a few fancy yachts.

He'd defended her.

Really defended her.

After the shark incident he'd been much more attentive at the lab, but she'd felt his attention had been motivated more because he knew the work mattered to her than by the fact that the work itself was important. In other words, she'd felt a little as if he was humoring her. After their dive this morning, she'd seen a change in that attitude, but she hadn't realized how much of a change.

He got it. Totally. He one hundred percent understood why she did what she did. More than that, he respected it.

And he respected her for doing it.

Warm fuzzies washed through her. And something, something that had been missing, slid into place.

Her parents' front door slammed.

She turned to see Brady coming down the stairs, a rifle case in each hand. She smiled and shook her head. "Don't you think that's overkill?"

He shook his head, moving around the front of the car and opening the door on the driver's side. "After this afternoon, I'd like to have a couple of bazookas. But since these were the most effective weapons your dad had, they'll have to do." He placed them carefully in the back seat, then crawled into the driver's seat, his green-eyed gaze meeting hers. "I convinced your dad I could protect you with them." He nodded to the guns in the back. "Or would you prefer to stay here where there's real security?"

She shook her head. "I can't stay."

"Look, Laura, if this is about the fight you and your dad—"

"It's not about the fight, Brady." *It's about us.* But she couldn't say that. She'd never been to bed with a man in her life. She didn't have the first clue how to go about setting up a seduction. But she was pretty sure it shouldn't be done in her family's house with her parents wandering around. Beyond that, she was going to have to make it up as she went along.

She pulled her legs in and shut the door behind her. "Just take us home, Brady. Take us home."

Thirteen

Laura climbed the stairs to her house, her heart pounding, her palms sweating and her tummy trilling with anxiety and anticipation. How *did* one go about seducing a man? Well, not seducing, really. She didn't think Brady was going to need much persuasion, thank God, because a full-out seduction was definitely beyond her very limited experience. This would be more like giving him a green light. She thought she could manage that, though she wasn't quite sure how.

She unlocked her door and entered her house.

Brady followed, carrying both rifle cases. "Do you want me to bring the dive gear in, get it rinsed off?"

She shook her head. "It can wait. Let's…have a drink. I could definitely use a drink."

"After the day we've had, a drink sounds good." He set the cases down by the sofa.

She went to the fridge and rummaged around. Pepsi, milk… Yeah, there it was. She pulled out a bottle of champagne she'd had chilling for…well, months.

Brady eyed the bottle skeptically. "You don't happen to have anything stronger lying around, do you?''

"As a matter of fact, I do. Holt comes by occasionally, and he's not much of a bubbly wine drinker, either.'' She pulled the bottle of Crown Royal out of her cupboard. "This okay?''

He smiled. "Absolutely.''

She grabbed a highball glass, then on second thought grabbed two. He was right, this moment definitely called for something stronger than champagne. She poured them both a couple of fingers. "Do you want ice?''

He shook his head. "And dilute this heavenly mash? No way.''

She handed him his glass and downed a giant swallow of hers in a single, determined gulp. Fire raced down her throat, exploded in her belly and sent tears streaming from her eyes. She coughed, sputtered, coughed again. "Okay, that was a little stronger than I anticipated.''

Brady chuckled. "Just give it a minute. You'll be fine. And you might want to try sipping the next bit. Beyond the fact you're obviously not used to hard liquor, inhaling this fine whiskey is a shame.''

She nodded, tapping her chest with her fist, trying to get her breath back. "Good idea.'' She let the warmth from the whiskey infuse her system and waited for it to bolster her nerve.

Brady took a sip of his own drink, his expression

turning serious. "Laura, you probably don't want to hear this, but I'm going to say it anyway."

"What?"

"I know you're mad at your parents right now. But I really think you need to talk this out with them. Soon."

"Stop." She held her hand up, forestalling his words. "Believe me, my parents are the last thing I want to talk about."

He cocked his head, studying her. "But from the way you said that, it sounds like there *is* something you want to talk about."

This was it. If she was going to do this, she wasn't going to get a better opening. "As a matter of fact, there is. I..." Oh God, was she brave enough to do this? She stared at the man standing not three feet from her. He was so handsome and charming and so...experienced. And she was so *not*.

She could make such a fool of herself.

But she'd never felt so completely accepted by a man before. He didn't want her money. Or his own little boat. He understood why she worked where she did. Was she going to miss out on all that?

She drew a deep breath and jumped into the abyss. "My middle name is Lynn."

He stilled, his gaze locking on to hers. "Lynn."

She nodded, her stomach clenching.

He set his glass down and closed the distance between them. He ran his finger down her arm, the heated touch raising goose bumps on her skin. He smiled that sexy smile she loved so much. But he made no other move. And after a moment he took his hand away and looked into her eyes. "Look, I don't want you to take this the wrong way, because I am more than interested in following this line of action. But…are you sure? It's been a hell of a day. And anyone with a degree in psychology or a modicum of sense can tell you life-threatening events can sometimes convince us to make decisions we wouldn't otherwise consider."

He was looking out for her. She smiled, shaking her head. "That's not what convinced me, Brady. It was… It was the way you defended me to my father. While you obviously aren't going to want to spend your life studying the ocean, you understand why I do. I think that's what I was waiting for. That validation. It's silly, I know. No one should have to validate my life but me. But it's nice to have someone understand." She shrugged. "It's like when you buy a great dress or get a great toy for Christmas. Just having the thing is nice. But it's *so* much nicer when others look at it and think it's as great as you do. You know what I mean?"

He smiled and touched her arm again, a soft, gentle, one-human-reaching-out-to-another touch. "I know what you mean."

The sadness, the loneliness in his eyes hit her hard. Of course, he understood. While she'd spent most of her life bemoaning the fact her parents didn't understand her, he'd spent his entire childhood and part of his young adulthood just wanting to be *noticed* by his.

She couldn't imagine how lonely that must have been. How terribly, terribly lonely. And now as an adult he'd committed himself to an equally lonely existence. Because he didn't want to risk hurting a woman the way his father had hurt his mother. His selflessness shamed her.

And made her want this night even more.

But not just for herself. For him, too. She wanted to chase that loneliness from his eyes. If only for a little while. She took his hand and led him toward her bedroom. "Come on, Brady. Let's get naked."

"Just a minute." He picked up his wallet from the counter and removed a condom from it.

Heat suffused her cheeks but she took his hand again and led him to the bedroom where her courage faltered a little. It was the middle of the day, she had nothing but sheers over her windows. There would be no darkness to hide either her body or her inexperienced fumbles.

Luckily, he took over, set the condom on the night stand and pulled her close, snuggling his hips against hers. And before she had a chance to get really nervous, his lips closed over hers, soft and warm and ohh…

She melted into him, soaking up his heat, the hard maleness of his body, the erotic persuasion of his kiss.

This kiss was nothing like the ones on the boat.

Those kisses had been angry and hard and eventually frantic.

But this… She could kiss like this all day.

His tongue pushed gently at the seam of her lips.

She opened to him, letting him in. He tasted like Crown Royal, hot male and heaven. She wanted this moment to go forever. She snuggled closer, stroking his body with hers.

He obliged, cupping her bottom and pulling their hips closer together, but only for a minute. Then he was pulling away.

She whimpered, grabbing his shoulders and going up on her toes to prolong the kiss.

He chuckled, low and sexy, pulling his lips from hers. "Hang in there. This is only going to get better. You did mention something about getting naked, didn't you?" His hands moved to the straps of her bathing suit, his fingers running along the flesh there. A subtle pause, a silent asking of permission.

When she made no objection, he slowly peeled the straps from her shoulders and pulled the swimsuit down to her waist, freeing her breasts. He inhaled, a hissing, reverent sound. "I can't tell you how many nights I dreamed of seeing you like this."

Heat washed over her, both from passion and embarrassment. No man had ever seen her naked before. "Is it better or worse than you imagined?"

He smiled, a cat-got-the-cream smile. "Oh, better. Much, much better." He touched her breasts. A soft, gentle touch. A tantalizing tease.

Her nipples peaked, and heat washed through her.

His gaze locked on her nipples. "It looks like you like that." He repeated the caress.

"Oh, yeah." Her voice was rough, breathy.

He looked up into her face. "Good. You'll like this even better."

He bent down and licked a nipple, his hot wet tongue flicking over the sensitive nub.

A small explosion went off inside her, sharp tingles shooting through her, starting at her breast and spreading outward, downward. She grabbed hold of his shoulders to support her suddenly weak knees. "Brady."

He looked up. "Austin. My name is Austin." He moved his head as if to repeat the touch, but he stopped short of her nipple, his tongue poised just millimeters from the tingling peak. He looked up, his eyes sparkling with mischief.

Her fingers bit into his shoulders. "Austin. Austin, Austin—"

His tongue flicked over her nipple again, hot and wet and...

Oh, my. Her knees gave out.

He scooped her up and carried her the few steps to her bed. After laying her down, he stripped her bathing suit off with one quick swipe. Then he divested himself of his swimming trunks with the same speed.

She stared at his pulsing sex, her mouth dry, her pulse scrambling to find a steady beat. Just as she'd never been seen naked by a man before, neither had she seen a naked man. She'd copped a quick peek at an Internet sex site once, but it was nothing like this. Nothing like the real thing. Brad— *Austin*'s broad shoulders, lean, hard muscles and more than generous sex made him one gorgeous, pulse-pounding, tummy-tingling hunk.

"Having fun?"

She snapped her eyes up, heat scalding her cheeks. But when she realized there was nothing but mischief and male pride in his eyes, she laughed. "As a matter of fact, I am." It was a scary kind of fun, trying something a little bit risky for the first time, but it was definitely fun.

That low, sexy chuckle filled the room. "Good." He lay down beside her, his hand stroking over her body, his gaze following his touch. He started at her collarbone, his fingers light and feather soft. Then he drifted down to her breasts, where the path became twisted and curved as it traced a lazy pattern.

She arched beneath his touch, heat and need gathering like clouds before a storm, making the air heavy and supercharged.

It was a little unnerving lying naked beside a man while he touched her, watched her. She was tempted to close her eyes, but it would be closing him out. And she didn't want to do that. She had the feeling that Austin Brady had spent a lot of his life on the outside looking in. She wanted him to know she was a hundred percent with him on this adventure.

She reached out, her hands a little shaky but determined. His skin was hot and smooth, the muscle beneath hard. Nice. Very nice. She tested the width of his shoulders, then ran her hands down over his chest. His nipples hardened beneath her hands. His sex flexed against her hip. Surprise zinged through her. Had her touch done that? She looked up.

He cocked a brow. "What? You think I'd be unaffected by your touch?"

Actually, she hadn't known what to expect. But she didn't think she'd tell him that. She didn't want him to freak out about the virgin thing or get noble or anything else that might make him stop. "Let's just say the men in my past haven't been so enthusiastic." Of course, she'd never given them the chance. But that was her secret.

She copied his movements with her hands. If his fingers trailed lightly toward her nipples, she did the same to him, hoping that if whatever he did made her feel good, her touch would do the same for him.

It didn't take him long to catch on that he was being mimicked. Smiling wickedly, he trailed a single finger between her breasts and down to her navel, where he made slow, lazy circles, his expression teasing and sinfully sexy.

She trailed her finger down his breastbone, over his upper abdomen to the top of his navel. She stopped.

He held his breath.

Giving him a wicked smile of her own, she circled his navel, her finger coming so close...

He sucked in his breath, his sex flexing again.

Her breathing picked up a notch. She wanted to touch him there. Wanted to see if he was as hard as he looked. As hot as he looked. And with the slow ache building inside her, she wanted his touch to move lower, too.

He didn't disappoint her. His hand moved lower, lower... "Come on, Laura. Play fair. I'm not hiding anything from you. Open up."

Heat suffused her cheeks, but her knees opened almost of their own volition.

He touched her, his fingers stroking, stroking.

She gasped, arching against him, the slow ache turning into a sharp, coiling need. A need that tightened with each stroke. Tightened and tightened until she couldn't stand it anymore. She arched higher, needing more contact, begging for more contact.

He obliged.

She burst into a million, sparkling pieces. Moaning, she shuddered as wave after wave of fire and ice rolled over her. His hand slowed and then moved away from her core all together, resting quietly on her thigh. She looked up at him, her breath coming in short, hard gasps, amazement sliding through her.

He looked down at her with a teasing grin. "Hairtrigger, huh?"

She laughed softly. "So it would appear." She'd never felt anything so incredible in her life. She felt like every nerve in her body was alive and dancing. And she wanted to make him feel just as good. "Let's see if you're any better." She reached down.

He grabbed her wrist before she reached her goal, shaking his head, a wry smile turning up his lips. "At the moment I'm not any further away from release than you were. And I want to be a part of you when I fly apart."

She wanted that, too. And before she could get nervous about the event, he sheathed himself in the latex protection, moved over her, took her mouth with his, nudged her knees apart and sank into her.

A stinging pain shot through her. She sucked in a sharp breath, her fingers digging into his back.

He stilled, his body snapping tight as a bow. Raising himself on his elbows, he stared down at her. "Laura? Was that what I think it was?" He took in her pained expression. "It *was*." He started to disengage.

She closed her arms around his shoulders. "Don't go anywhere. Just…give me a minute."

He stilled again, dropping his head beside her shoulder. "Why didn't you tell me?"

"Because I didn't want you to do what you're trying to do now. Pull away."

He gently rubbed her shoulder, the touch gentle but sad somehow. "It might have been better, Laura."

She hated the regret in his voice. "No, it wouldn't have been. I want you here. In my bed. In *me*."

He raised his head, his eyes meeting hers. "Why did you decide to go for broke now? Why with me?"

She cocked her head, studying him. "You make it sound like this wasn't a good choice."

"I'm not sure it was."

She shifted beneath him, trying to ease the dull ache, but it was the concern in his expression that held her attention. "Because you won't be staying?"

He nodded, pushing a strand of hair from her face. "I don't want to hurt you. Isn't a woman's first time supposed to be special? I'm just some bum who wandered into your life for a few weeks."

She smiled, running her fingers through his hair, studying his face, memorizing it. "You are a lot of things, Austin Brady, but a bum isn't one of them. You have—bar none—the best heart of any man I've ever met. Of any*one* I've ever met."

He looked at her as if she'd lost her mind. "Laura, I'm a selfish, freewheeling, take-what-I-can-get-and-run bastard."

She laughed softly. "You're nothing of the kind. You're a man who cares about children—and tries to make their world better. A man who cares whether a daughter gets along with her parents. A man who has spent most of his life alone—despite the fact I think it isn't exactly what he wants—because he's afraid of hurting someone else. That's not my definition of a selfish bastard."

"You're taking a few disjointed facts and romanticizing them."

"Then let me romanticize." She ran her fingers through his hair again. "Listen, we've both had our share of dark, lonely nights. Me, because I don't want a man who's more interested in my money and an Evans yacht than he is in me. You, because you're afraid your itchy feet don't make good long-term relationship material. Fine. We both have our crosses to bear. But we don't have to bear them tonight. The first night you were here, you promised me a nerve-shatteringly, mind-blowingly good memory. I want that, Austin. I *want* that memory, for all the dark, lonely nights ahead of both of us."

His gaze darkened with longing. "I want it, too."

"Good." The dull ache gone, she shifted beneath him again, this time marveling at the fullness he created within her. "Then show me how this is done."

His gaze darkened even more. "Absolutely." He sipped at her lips. "Pain gone?"

She nodded. "Now I just feel full…and tingly." She shivered against him, that hungry tightening starting all over again.

He smiled that slow, sexy smile. "That's the way we like it." He slowly started moving, his body stroking hers, his hardness retreating and then thrusting deep.

His strokes were long.

Slow.

His gaze dark.

Hooded.

But it was locked on hers as they climbed up…
And up.
And over…
Together.

Fourteen

"You've set up a meeting with the rebel leader in Ivory Coast?" Austin sat on one of the tall stools at the counter in Laura's kitchen the next morning, talking to the managing editor at *Time*. "No, that'll be fine. Book the ticket. I'm done here." He snapped his cell phone closed and checked his watch.

The flight out of the U.S. left at two this afternoon. It was already nine now. If he was going to make his flight he needed to get moving. By the time he packed, got Laura to her parents' house, drove an hour and a half to the airport and stood in line for two hours for the security check, he wouldn't have much time to waste.

But he didn't move.

For the first time in his life, the thought of moving on didn't hold the slightest appeal. Normally he was ready to move on before he'd gotten halfway through an article. But not this time. He shifted his gaze to the closed bedroom door. Laura was behind that door, sleeping. The thought of leaving her made his chest ache. But he had to go. He'd known it long before the sun had come up this morning. Long before he and Laura had quit testing each other's limits.

Heat slipped through his system just thinking about the past eighteen hours. About Laura's innocent responses, her unbridled enthusiasm and the infinite care with which she'd made love. He could easily get lost in her touch, her loving.

Too easily.

That was why he was hightailing it out of here now.

If he could just make himself get off this stool.

The bedroom door suddenly opened and Laura stood there, her hair tossed, her lips swollen from his kisses, her hazel eyes sated and sleepy. She started to smile when she spotted him sitting at the counter, but her lips had barely turned when she took in the look on his face and the cell phone he'd set on the counter. Her face fell. "Oh God, you're leaving, aren't you?" She crossed her arms protectively over her chest.

His stomach knotted, but there was no point in beating around the bush. "Yes."

She slumped against the doorjamb, pain and disappointment filling her expression. "You're running away."

"I'm not running away. I have an assignment. *Time* has arranged for me to interview the rebel leader in Ivory Coast."

She shot him a suspicious look. "Did they call you? Or did you call them?"

He grimaced.

"That's what I thought. You're afraid of what happened between us yesterday. And all night last night. And now you're running away.''

Hell yes, he was afraid. He'd made love to more than his share of women, but he'd *never* felt anything like what he and Laura had shared. Which is why it had gone on all afternoon.

And all evening.

And all damned night.

And it would still be going on now if Laura, thoroughly exhausted, hadn't fallen asleep just after the sun came up this morning. But, thankfully, she had gone to sleep. And he'd been able to think long enough to come to his senses and realize he had to leave. Immediately. Before they got in any deeper than they already were. He walked over to the sofa and started throwing his clothes in his duffel, ignoring her, hoping she'd make it easy on both of them and just drop the subject.

''You felt it, didn't you?''

So much for that hope. He could feel her eyes boring into his back. ''Felt what?''

''That there was more going on last night than sex.''

''Laura, don't analyze it to death. It's time for me to go. That's all.''

''That's not all, and you know it. You felt it, *didn't you?*

Damn. She was going to poke and prod until she got her answers. ''Yes, I felt it. Which is why I need to go. Now. Before our emotions become any more involved.''

''You mean before *my* emotions become more involved.''

''Yes.'' He felt like a complete bastard. He needed to go, but the last thing he wanted her to think was that any of this was her fault. He turned to her, the pair of shorts he was about to stick in his bag bunched in his hands. ''Look, if it's any consolation, I don't want to go. I want to stay. For the first time in my life I want to stay.''

She tossed her hands in the air. ''Then why are you leaving?''

''Because my wanting to stay won't last. And because you're not the type of woman who can be involved with a man for any length of time and not get hurt.''

''How do you know what type of woman I am?''

''You were a thirty-year-old virgin, Laura. It doesn't take a rocket scientist to know you're not going to take any involvement with a man lightly. I never should have—''

''Don't say that.'' She slashed her hand through the air. ''Last night was the most wonderful night of my life. I won't have you say it shouldn't have happened.'' Tears sprang into her eyes.

His stomach tightened another notch. He'd screwed up. Big time. He'd never meant to hurt her.

Blinking back the tears, she lifted her chin. ''How

do you know it won't last if you won't even give it a chance?''

It hurt too much to look at her tears. He turned away from her, shoving the shorts into his duffel. ''I know whose son I am. No matter how much I might want that to change, it isn't going to.''

''You're not your father.''

''I'm just like him. Neither of us were built for staying in one place. He needed the rush bright lights and fast women gave him. I need the rush an adrenaline high gives me.''

''Why? What does that rush give you?''

He plowed his fingers through his hair. It was a question he didn't like to look at too closely.

''What, Austin? What does it give you?''

He went into the bathroom, collecting his things, willing her to drop the subject.

But she moved in front of the bathroom and planted herself like a warrior. ''I deserve an answer, and I'm not going anywhere until you give me one.''

Dammit. ''Because it fills a hole in me, all right? It's the only time I feel...whole.'' He pushed past her, striding back to the couch.

''And you didn't feel whole last night? Because I've got to tell you, I've never felt so complete.''

''Last night was wonderful, but, then, it was one adrenaline rush after another. But that won't last, Laura. It can't. And then where will we be?'' He tossed his shaving gear into his duffel. ''I'll tell you where. More emotionally involved when my feet start itching and the drive to move pushes me to my next destination. I'm not going to do that to you. I'm not going to do it to us. My leaving now is best. I know it. And if you'd think it through you'd know it, too.''

''What about the article?''

It was a last-ditch effort, and they both knew it.

He gentled his voice. ''It's almost done. And I have the information I need to finish it. If I need more, I'll call. But I don't imagine that will happen.'' He locked his gaze on hers. ''It will be a good article, Laura.''

The best damned article he'd ever written.

She slumped onto the sofa next to his duffel and swiped at another tear. ''I'm not going to change your mind about this, am I?''

He shook his head, resisting the urge to pull her into his arms with every ounce of willpower he had.

''In the past I thought this rule you had about not getting involved in relationships was noble. Today I just think it sucks.''

''It does suck. But it's still the right choice.''

She looked away from him, plowing a hand through her hair and wiping at the tears that managed to get away.

He'd give anything to be able to leave her be. Let her deal with her hurt in peace. But there was one more blow he had to deliver. ''I want you to throw whatever you need into a bag to stay at your parents' place for the next little bit. I called them earlier and told them I'd be bringing you by."

Her gaze snapped to his. "What?"

"I can't leave you here all alone. Not after yesterday. It's not safe. Your dad and mom agree. They're waiting for you."

"Well, here's a news flash for you—and my folks. I'm way past the age of consent. It doesn't matter what my parents—or you—think, I get to make my own decisions. And I am *not* going to my parents'."

"Unfortunately, it's not that easy. Here are your choices—either you go there, where you can move around fairly unfettered in the security of your folks' estate or your dad's sending three armed guards to dog your every move here."

She glared at him as if he was the lowest form of slug.

"Sorry. I know it's not what you want. But there's no option here. Not with DeBruzkya's men out there."

She shoved off the sofa and stalked toward her bedroom. "This totally sucks, Brady."

Didn't he know it.

Laura sat in the passenger seat of Austin's rental car, her heart aching, tears still threatening to pour down her cheeks. Why was she so bad at this man—woman thing? Every time she put her hat in the ring, it got smashed flatter than a pancake before it even had a chance.

For the thousandth time since they'd left her driveway, not two minutes ago, he glanced in her direction. "I'm sorry, Laura. More sorry than you can imagine."

She sniffed, trying to ignore the pain in her chest, trying to be an adult about all this. "Why are you sorry? You're not the one who broke your rules. I am." And she would do it again, because—

No. No, no, *no.* She wasn't going to go there.

She wasn't.

But it was too late. She was already there. All she had to do was feel the ache in her chest or listen to the silent cries echoing in her head.

Dear God, she loved him.

She dropped her head back against the headrest and stared at the beige upholstered ceiling. Now what? Was she just going to sit here like a sniveling ninny and let him walk out of her life? She rolled her head, looking over at him.

He didn't look any happier than she felt. He shot another sideways look at her. "Don't start, Laura. This is the right choice."

"I disagree."

"I know you do. But it's not going to change anything. I know who I am. I know what I'm capable of, and what I'm not capable of. I'm not going to hang around any longer, making this harder on both of us." He pulled into her parents' driveway, swiped the security card he'd asked for earlier and drove through the gate.

She stared at him, anger and frustration boiling

inside her. "I think you're making a mistake." She held her hand up, forestalling his objection. "I know I'm not going to change your mind, but I'm going to say this, whether you want to hear it or not. I don't know anything about itchy feet or adrenaline rushes. I can't say whether a life-threatening thrill can fill a hole in anyone or not. But I do know when I look at you, when I look in your eyes, I see a loneliness there that breaks my heart. And that, I can fill." She held her breath, hoping, praying her words would make him reconsider.

He looked away, his lips pressing into a hard, thin line. Silence filled the car as he drove up to her parents' front door. Putting the car in park, he turned to her, his green eyes as dull and desolate as she'd ever seen them. "Do you want me to help you with your bag?"

Her heart squeezed. He wasn't going to be swayed. He was leaving. No matter how hard it was for either of them. And right now she thought it was as hard for him as it was for her. He believed he was doing what was best for both of them.

Pain slicing through her, she managed to shake her head. "I can get it. Thanks, anyway." Turning from him, she pulled the door's handle and swung it open. But she couldn't get out. Not yet. Not without one final touch.

She leaned over and kissed him on the cheek, drinking in his warmth and smell and sweetness one last time. "Be well, Austin Brady. Take care of you."

Fifteen

Seconds later, Laura stood in the driveway, looking at her parents. They were waiting for her on the porch, standing next to each other in their usual solidarity. With emptiness sweeping over her like a cold wave, Laura envied them that. They were lucky to have each other.

Their expressions were apprehensive. Not unexpected after the argument they'd had on the boat yesterday. She should feel the same apprehension, but she didn't. Truth be told, despite her initial reaction about being ushered to her family's place like a child who couldn't take care of herself, she was glad to be here. Her place would seem far too empty without Austin.

Doing her best to appear normal, she drew a deep breath, lifted her chin and climbed the stairs.

She hadn't made it to the top step before concern knitted her mother's brow. "Laura, honey, are you okay?"

So much for appearing normal. She should have known better. Mom was hard to fool. But she was going to give it another go, anyway. She affected a shrug. "I'm fine, Mom."

Her mother didn't looked convinced.

And her father's eyes narrowed on her. "If you're angry about my insistence that you either come here or I send guards to your place, I'm sorry. But after yesterday I think it's clear we're all in danger until this mess is cleared up. I don't want you there alone."

That was the last thing she wanted to fight about. She waved away his concerns. "It's okay, Dad. I don't mind."

"Okay, now I know something's wrong." Her mother's gaze honed in on her as only a mother's can. "Are you still upset about what happened yesterday?"

She wished that's all it was. "No, Mom. I'm fine. Really."

Her mother's expression clearly said she didn't believe her. "If you're not upset about yesterday, what is upsetting you? Did Austin do something?"

"I told you, I'm fine." But just the sound of his name brought tears to her eyes, and before she could blink them back one slipped by. She swiped at it, forcing a smile. "Allergies. They've been driving me crazy lately."

"Laura Lynn, you've never had an allergy in your life." Her mother looked at her, then looked out to where Austin was pulling out of the security gates, then back to Laura. "It's Austin, isn't it?"

"Mother, just let it go."

Her mother cocked her head, studying her. "Were you two getting close?"

She wanted to deny it, but her throat was too tight to answer, and the fresh tears stinging her eyes made a liar of her, anyway.

"Oh, honey." Her mother closed her in her arms.

Laura soaked in her mother's warmth and comfort.

Her mom gave her a tight squeeze. "Come on, let's go in and you can tell me what happened." Her mother herded her through the house into the ocean room, her father following.

Her mother waved toward the sofa. "Have a seat. I'll have Jeanne make us some tea." She headed off to the kitchen.

Her dad sat down beside her, putting his arm around her and pulling her close. "If those tears are any indication, it looks like you two were more than getting close. It looks like you were pretty involved."

"I think I love him." She shook her head. "How could that happen in such a short time?"

His expression turned wry. "With your mother it happened to me in a day."

She swiped at a stray tear. "Really?"

He nodded. "But I was lucky. She returned my feelings. I can't imagine what I would have done if she hadn't." But the look in his eyes clearly said he would have been devastated.

Which was exactly how she felt. Devastated. She leaned against her father, accepting his support.

He smoothed her hair back from her face. "Want me to send Holt and Seth after him? Let him know I don't like anyone hurting my daughter?"

His automatic support sent warmth through her. She chuckled and shook her head, sniffing back her tears. "Thanks, anyway. But I don't want to hurt him. I think he carries enough pain around with him as it is."

She thought of Austin driving off—alone—heading for a war zone where there would be neither comfort nor understanding.

Until this moment she hadn't realized what a boon her parents' love was. Or how much she'd taken it for granted. She took hold of her father's hand, pulling his arm, his protective embrace a little closer.

Her father smiled down at her. "You know, I've been thinking about what your reporter said yesterday, about your job, and—"

"Dad, let's not talk about that now, okay? I'm beginning to think it doesn't matter. Which doesn't mean I plan on coming to work at Evans Yachts," she quickly amended. "I don't. But it does mean I'm not going to fight with you about it anymore. Austin was right. Family is too important to let minor squabbles blow it apart. The important thing is, you love me. And I love you and Mom. If you don't understand my work, you don't understand it. I'll learn to live with that."

Her father hugged her. "That's nice to hear, sweetie, but your mother and I spent last evening discussing Brady's astuteness ourselves. I realized that one reason I wanted all my children to work at Evans Yachts was because I loved it so much. Being able to pass that joy on to my children was always a dream of mine."

She raised a brow. "And it didn't occur to you that some of your children might not love it?"

He laughed, a self-deprecating chuckle. "No, it never did. Especially since two of them love it as much as I did."

"And you figured I was just being stubborn."

He raised a patriarchal brow. "It *is* in your nature."

She smiled. "Yes, it is. But I'm not just being stubborn about my work, Dad. I love it."

He nodded. "I'm beginning to understand that. I guess I'm a little slow. Your mom caught on a while ago, and she's been trying to convince me."

"Smart lady."

"The smartest one he knows," her mother said, striding back into the living room, cups of tea in hand. Giving one to Laura, she sat back down and sipped at the other cup. "Did your father tell you we'd like to go down with you and see what it is you study all day?"

How many years had she been waiting to hear those words? Joy washed through her.

"That is, if you think you can teach a couple old fogies like us how to scuba," her dad said.

"I'll have you breathing underwater in no time.

Thanks, Dad. And you, too, Mom. I can't tell you what this means to me.''

And it was all a gift from Austin.

Fresh tears threatened to spill. She blinked away the ones she could and dashed the others with a quick swipe.

"It means just as much to us." Her father gave her another squeeze, dropped a kiss on her brow and stood. "I'll take your bag up to your room and leave you and your mother to talk. If I hear too much about Brady, I probably will have to get a gun and go after the man," he observed sardonically, grabbing the bag and heading for the stairs.

Laura forced herself to take a sip of tea as she stared out at the ocean, thinking of Austin, feeling bruised and raw and numb.

As if sensing Laura's need to sort through her feelings, her mother sat with her, offering nothing more than silent support.

The phone rang, the sound a rude reminder that the rest of the world was in full swing around her.

Her mother stood and crossed the room.

Laura thought about going on up to her room. She wouldn't have to be brave there. She could cry all she wanted. But her limbs felt too heavy to move. And she was afraid if she really started crying she might never stop. So she stayed where she was, watching the waves roll in and then back out to sea. Her mother's voice droned on behind her, but Laura didn't pay any attention. The world might still be functioning outside these walls, but inside them Laura definitely wasn't.

A few minutes later her mother walked over to her, phone in hand. "It's your cousin Honey. She wants to talk to you."

Laura panicked. "Oh God, you didn't tell her about Austin, did you?"

"No, I didn't. And you don't have to whisper, I have the phone on mute. I did mention you were here and she said she wanted to talk to you. Since you two girls always seem to cheer each other up, I thought it would be a good idea." Her mother handed Laura the phone. "I'll just go get us more tea while you talk." With that lame excuse, obviously cooked up to give Laura time to talk to Honey privately, she disappeared.

Laura stared at the phone in her hands. The last thing she felt like doing was making small talk. But there was no way out now. She pushed the mute button to deactivate the feature and held the phone to ear. "Hi, Honey. How are you feeling?" Her cousin was nearing the end of her first pregnancy.

"Right as rain. How are you? Your mom says you're not feeling well."

Laura grimaced. "Just a cold."

"Yeah, you sound pretty stuffed up."

Laura nodded to herself and tried to think of something to say. "So, are you going to have that baby in time to bring him or her to the regatta? I can't wait to see your new addition."

"You can't wait to *hold* the baby. I know you."

Laura made a halfhearted attempt at a laugh. "You're right. Are you coming?"

"Absolutely. I can't wait to congratulate big brother, Drew, on his engagement to Alison and welcome her into the family in person."

"They'll be glad to see you. And—" The phone line crackled while Laura struggled to come up with more small talk. "And...so will I."

"Laura, are you all right?"

A silent groan echoed through Laura's head. Honey had the best something's-wrong radar in the universe. Somehow she had to deflect it. "Except for this cold, I'm fine."

"Uh-huh. I'm not buying it. You sound like you have more than a stuffy nose. You sound...depressed. What's wrong, girl? Are you and your family fighting over your work again?"

Laura sighed. Honey wouldn't give up until she knew exactly what was going on. "No, actually, I think we've finally worked that out."

"Really? That's great. Really great. But if you're not fighting with your parents, what's making you so sad?"

"Honey, I don't want to talk about it right now, okay?"

"Uh-oh, it's a man, isn't it?"

Laura stared at the ceiling and injected as much don't-be-ridiculous tone as she could muster into her voice. "What makes you think it's a man?"

"Oh God, it *is*. The only time you use that stupid tone of voice is when you're trying to throw me off the scent. And I'm guessing you don't have a cold, either, you little liar. You're all stuffed up because he made you cry. What's his name? I'll track him down and peel his skin off inch by inch."

Laura laughed, a strangled, watery affair. "That's my Honey. Ever the sweet little savage avenger. But as much as I appreciate your offer, I'd rather you leave this one alone."

More static crackled over the line.

"Oh dear, this one was serious, wasn't he?"

Laura sighed. "It doesn't matter what it was. It's over."

"If it was that great, Laura, if *he* was that great, don't give up on him. It wasn't easy for Max and me, either. We went through hell. But in the end, we worked it out. And look at us now. There's no happier couple on earth."

Fresh pain slashed through Laura as she thought about all the happy couples around her. Honey and Max. Drew and Alison. Seth and Emma. Hell, all the Proteans had managed to fall in love and get married despite their troubles. But Laura Evans? No way. "You were lucky, Honey. Max hung around long enough for you two to work it out. But there won't be any working things out for Austin and me. He's gone. And he's not coming back."

Sixteen

Austin raced from the blackened hull of the burned-out car toward the low stone wall, zigzagging as bullets flew in every direction around him. He slid in the last few feet, like a base runner stealing second, and crouched beneath the wall.

The two rebel soldiers who were escorting him back to his plane after his four-day interview with the rebel leader skidded in beside him.

Breathing hard, adrenaline pouring through him, Austin waited for the thrill of the moment to overtake him.

It didn't happen.

It hadn't happened on this entire godforsaken trip. And there had certainly been every opportunity for the old thrill to kick in. He'd barely escaped an ambush meant for the rebel leader he'd come to interview, he'd had a close encounter with a stinger missile and he'd dodged enough bullets to gag a hippo. Exactly the kind of stuff he usually ate up. The kind of stuff that usually filled that hole inside him.

But this time around it had neither filled the hole nor seemed particularly thrilling. If anything, the emptiness inside him had been sharper since he'd left

Laura. The life-threatening moments that usually sent that rush of excitement through him just seemed... annoying. He wanted to wrap this damned story up and get back to...

Get back to Laura.

He sat against the short stone wall, and lowered his head against the hard surface. Sporadic gunfire sounding around him, he stared up at the African sky and mumbled to himself, "Get over it, Brady. You're not going back to Laura."

But heaven help him, he wanted to go back to her.

His every waking moment—hell, his every sleeping moment, too—was filled with images of Laura. Laura giving him hell for ignoring her precious ocean. Laura lying in her bed at night in her soft, cotton pajamas. Laura, naked as the day she was born, wrapped around him and hugging him tight. He wanted her back.

A bullet skimmed over the top of the wall, sending shards of rock spraying in every direction. He closed his eyes, keeping the dust out and trying to focus on the moment at hand. Sitting in the middle of a fire-fight was not the time to let one's attention wander.

He peeked over the wall, trying to get an estimate of how many gunmen had them pinned down. Crouching back down, he looked to the rebel soldier next to him. "I counted four of them. How about you?"

The big African next to him nodded, his black skin glistening with sweat in the heat and humidity.

Since Austin didn't have a gun, that made his two rebel soldiers against the four government ones. Great. He raised a brow. "Any ideas on how we're going to get out of here?"

The rebel peeked over the wall, got shot at for his trouble, ducked back down and thought for a moment. "We're not going to be able to shoot our way out. But the airstrip is a mile down this road. Your plane should be waiting. You go. We'll keep them pinned down here. When we hear the plane take off, we'll sneak out the way we came."

Austin nodded. "Sounds like a plan to me." Now all he had to do was make it to the airstrip in one piece. And without being captured by the government soldiers shooting at them. If the editor he was working with at *Time* didn't hear from him by tonight, he'd send people looking for him. But Austin hated to think of the unpleasant hours he could spend as the government's "guest" while they tried to squeeze the rebel leader's whereabouts out of him before rescue could arrive. Wiping the sweat from his palms, he looked to the two rebels sitting in the dirt beside him. "Give me some cover fire."

They both nodded.

"On three," the soldier next to him said.

Austin got to his feet. Crouching low, he picked out the next bit of cover, a small bunch of trees about twenty-five feet away, and prepared to run.

The rebels readied their weapons. "One, two,

three.'' They rose up and began shooting over the wall.

Heart pounding, Austin started to run.

He zigged.

And zagged.

Two more steps and he'd be at the trees.

Something slammed into him from behind, knocking him to his knees. Searing pain slashed through his shoulder.

Son of bitch. He'd been shot.

He tried to push to his feet. He had to make it to that plane, dammit. But the pain slashed through him again.

The world went black.

Seventeen

Laura lay on the bed and stared up at the ceiling in the room she'd grown up in. It had been over two weeks since Austin had left. She should be feeling better, but she wasn't. She'd never felt so lonely or desolate in her life.

Her family had been great, rallying around her, trying to cheer her up. And she'd thrown herself into her research, working longer and harder than ever in an effort to push thoughts of Austin out of her mind. But the effort had been wasted. Like a remora stuck on a shark, his image was with her every step of the day, reminding her just how close she'd come to heaven. Reminding her just how alone she was now. She wasn't sure she would ever feel whole again.

"Laura?" Her mother's voice crackled over the intercom.

Sighing, Laura moved her head to stare at the small box next to her bedroom door. She wasn't up to facing people right now. She just wanted to lie here and stare at the ceiling and be miserable in peace.

"Laura, there's someone here to see you."

With another sigh she looked down at her pajamas.

She wasn't dressed for company. Which, since it was almost noon, was pretty pitiful. But it was Sunday and she wasn't up to dressing today. She definitely wasn't up to visitors.

She rolled off the bed and plodded to the intercom, shaking her head. She pushed the talk button. "Tell whoever it is I'm not up to visitors today."

"I already tried to get him to go away. He refuses." Irritation sounded in her mother's voice.

Laura scowled at the intercom. He? She couldn't imagine who it would be. But whoever it was, she'd send him on his way quickly enough. "Fine. I'll be right down."

Grabbing her robe from its hook on the door, she pulled it on and headed down the hall, tying the belt as she went.

At the end of the hall, she started down the stairs, looking over the wrought iron railing for the little cockroach. Her mother and he were standing—

Her heart stopped. She stumbled to a halt. Grabbing the rail for support, she stared down at the man standing in the entryway with her mother. "Austin?"

He looked up, his dear, dear face tight and a little anxious. "Laura."

She wasn't seeing things. He was really standing down there with her mother. She raced down the stairs, her gaze flying over him.

He looked so good. So tall and strong and— There was a sling on his shoulder.

"Oh God, you're hurt? What happened?" She

hurried to his side and ran her hand down his uninjured shoulder, reassuring herself that he was all right.

"Just a little accident. I'm fine." He was smiling now and seemed as happy to see her as she was to see him. His gaze skated over her from the top of her head to the tips of her toes. "You look good, Laura. Really good."

She laughed. "For pity's sake, Austin, I'm wearing crumpled pajamas, a ratty old robe and I haven't brushed my hair or—"

"You look good to me."

She stopped her list of imperfections, pleasure stealing through her. But a little wave of apprehension followed on its heels. When he left she didn't think she'd ever hear from him or see him again, and yet, here he was. She cocked her head. "What are you doing here? Do you have some more questions about the article? Do you need a place to stay while you heal?"

Her stomach clenched at the thought. She wasn't sure she could spend any amount of time with him. She'd only fall more in love with him. And if that happened she'd never survive watching him walk away again.

Her heart ached just thinking about it. And yet…if he wanted to stay, she'd let him. And she'd take care of him for as long as he needed her. For the first time she understood Austin's mother's situation. It wasn't a good place to be.

As if sensing her thoughts, the tightness and apprehension stole back into his face. "I don't need a place to heal. I came back because I need to talk to you."

"About what?"

He glanced to her mother, a hint of red crawling up his neck. "I'd like to speak to her alone, Mrs. Evans. If you don't mind."

Laura raised her brows. Mrs. Evans? But one look at her mother's face and Laura understood why Austin had been so formal. Her mother was in full-protective mode, her expression as dark and threatening as any mama bear's could be.

"It's okay, Mom," Laura reassured, giving her mom a little smile. "If I need someone to claw his eyes out, I'll holler."

Her mother returned her smile, but then turned to Austin, narrowing her eyes on him. "If you hurt her again, Mr. Brady, I'm going to send my husband and boys after you. Understand?"

"Yes, ma'am."

Her mother issued a final warning glance, then strode away.

Laura waved a hand toward the big double doors to her right. "Do you want to go into the ocean room and sit? You look a little pale." And he was getting paler by the moment.

"The ocean room sounds great."

Laura led the way, closing the doors behind them. Austin made his way to the sofa. "Since you're still here, I take it our nasty little dictator DeBruzkya is still after the sub plans.''

"Everyone thinks so. Unfortunately, we don't have enough proof.'' She joined him on the couch and gave him a serious look. "Enough about De-Bruzkya. I want to talk about you.'' Sitting next to him in the bright room, she could easily to see the paleness of his skin, the lines of pain around his eyes. He might be saying he was fine, but he was hurting. She tipped her head toward his shoulder. "What happened?''

He grimaced. "I lost a race with a bullet. But it's fine now. Nothing to worry about.''

Her blood crashed to her toes. "Shot? How can you possibly be fine? You've only been gone a little over two weeks. That bullet wound has to be pretty fresh. Shouldn't you still be in the hospital?''

He smiled. "I just got out of the hospital in Ghana. And I—''

"Ghana? I thought you were going to Ivory Coast?''

"That's where I was shot. But since it was a government soldier who shot me, the rebel soldiers escorting me thought it best not to leave me in the government's care. They managed to get me to my plane and had the pilot fly me to a hospital in Ghana. And believe me, getting out of that hospital was the best thing I could have done for my health.''

She cringed. "I don't even want to think about it. Did you check in with your doctor here?''

"I will."

She could picture him running from an armed soldier. Picture him falling when the bullet hit him. She ran a shaky hand through her hair. "Look, I know you love this adrenaline-pumping stuff, but you've got be more careful."

"I've been giving that a great deal of thought lately."

"Yeah? Since when?"

"Since I spent four days in Ivory Coast dodging bullets and missiles and government soldiers and got not one ounce of thrill for my trouble."

She gave him a wry look. "I can imagine getting shot could put a damper on things."

He shook his head. "I wasn't having any fun *before* I got shot."

That caught her attention. "Really?"

"Not a bit."

A spark flickered inside her. She squelched it and took hold of her rapidly escalating hopes. For all she knew he was here to talk about the article. She might be setting herself up for another crushing disappointment. She wasn't up to that. "So…why do you think you couldn't catch the usual high?"

"That was the question I kept asking myself. And it was damned frustrating. But being stuck in a community hospital room that had plenty of heat, humidity and misery but not a single TV or radio gave me plenty of time to think it through."

"And what did you find?"

"That the adrenaline rushes weren't filling that hole inside me, after all."

The spark flickered into a flame. "No?"

He shook his head. "They never had—they were only masking it. It's pretty hard to concentrate on anything else but survival when you're trying to stay alive."

"I imagine it is." She held her breath, waiting for him to continue.

"And once I realized that, the rest fell into place."

"And what was the rest?" she prodded, hoping, praying for an answer that would give him back to her.

"That my itchy feet weren't caused by a need to get to the next big rush at all. Nor were they a genetic inheritance from my father. I don't know why my father was always on the move, but I finally figured out why I was."

He hesitated, but then plowed ahead. "I was looking for a home. A real home like I'd always dreamed of as a child. One filled with love. It was that lack of love that left the hole inside me, the emptiness." He stood and paced away, plowing his fingers through his hair.

When he turned back to her, he met her gaze squarely. "You fill that hole, Laura. With your sweetness and passion and caring heart. You fill it."

She wanted to throw herself into his arms. But she resisted, clenching her fists in her lap, unwilling to get ahead of herself. She needed to know what this meant. What it was he wanted.

He strode back to the sofa and sat beside her. "I can't give up my profession. I love it, just like you love yours. The kids are important to me—you were right about that. But there's a lot I can do to help kids from right here in the U.S.A. Which doesn't mean I want to give up my war stories all together. I don't," he quickly amended. "But I can space them out so I won't be gone too much."

Excitement bubbled through her. "That sounds good." Very good.

He nodded, taking her hand. "I want you back, Laura. I want what we had together. I can't promise you I'm going to be very good at this relationship thing. But if you give me a chance, I'll get better. I promise. Lying in that hospital bed, I realized it wasn't that my dad left so often that made my mom sad. Made me sad. It was that he didn't love us. But I love you, Laura. *You.* Not your money or family's boats—you. And I'll make sure that every hour, every minute, every second of every day you know it. If you'll just give us a chance."

The joy exploded, sending tears cascading down her cheeks and love gushing from her heart.

He loved her.

Being careful not to hurt his injured arm, she threw her arms around his neck and hung on. "I love you, too. I knew it the day you left, but I didn't tell you. I should have. Oh God, I should have."

He squeezed her tight. "Telling me wouldn't have done any good. I was hell-bent on leaving. But I'm equally hell-bent on staying now. On making this work. I want it, Laura. I want you by my side in that hot little house by the sea. And I want a dozen kids to raise in it."

She pulled back. "Kids?" she squeaked.

He smiled. "You must think I'm getting a little ahead of myself."

She laughed. "Maybe a little."

"Well, this might help." He gently pulled her arms from his neck, reached into his sling and pulled out a gold ring. Sunlight streaming into the room glinted off the yellow metal. "Laura Evans, I love you. And I want to spend the rest of my life with you. Loving you. Cherishing you. Creating a home and family and life with you. Will you marry me?"

Tears gushed from her eyes. She swiped at them, a fullness she'd never felt before stretching her heart and soul. "Yes." She threw her arms around him again, hugging him close. "Yes, yes, *yes*."

"You're both getting way ahead of yourselves," her father's voice boomed.

Laura spun around to find her parents standing just inside the doorway that led from the ocean room to the formal dining room. "Oh no, I shut the big doors but I forgot about that entrance. How long have you two been standing there?"

"Long enough." Her father shifted his gaze to

Austin. "It's customary, Mr. Brady, to ask the lady's father for her hand in marriage before you propose."

Laura sighed. "That's a little old-fashioned, don't you think, Dad?

"No, he's right." Austin gave her hand a squeeze, then turned to her father. "Mr. Evans, I apologize for the breach in custom and respectfully ask for your daughter's hand in marriage."

Her father narrowed his eyes on Austin and raised his chin. "What if I were to say no?"

Laura groaned.

Austin laughed, a short, wry burst of sound. "I'm afraid you'd have to get used to me hanging around, asking you until you said yes."

Her father's expression didn't soften. If anything, his eyes narrowed a little more. "You made my daughter cry, Brady."

"Yes, sir, I did. You can't imagine how sorry I am about that. Or how hard I intend to work to make sure it never happens again."

"I'll hold you to that."

Austin's gaze never wavered. "I would expect you to."

"Then put the ring on her finger, boy. And let's open some champagne."

Austin turned to her, smiling from ear to ear.

She held her left hand out, trying to keep it steady.

He slid the ring to her knuckle, then locked his gaze on hers. "Every hour, every minute, every second. I love you, Laura Evans.'' He slipped the ring into place.

She leaned forward and kissed him, drinking in his warmth, reveling in the joy that bound them together. Then she pulled back, just enough to whisper against his lips. ''I'm going to fill that emptiness inside you, Austin. So full you won't know what to do with it.''

He kissed her—a deep, sensuous, you're-my-heart kiss. ''It's going to be good. Very, very good.''

She smiled through her tears. ''It's going to be…perfect.''

* * * * *

Don't miss the exciting conclusion to the
Family Secrets series,
RACING HEARTS
By
Lilian Darcy
In Emerald Cove, blood is thicker than water.

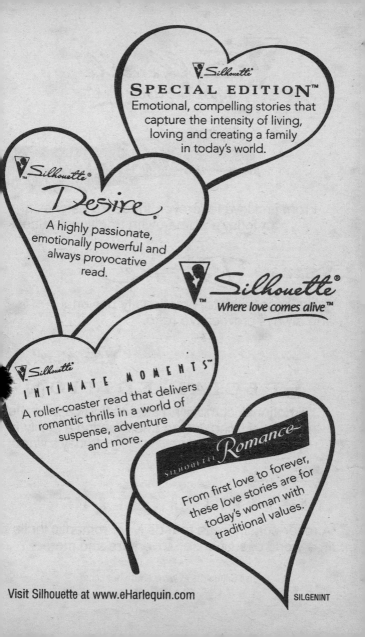

Silhouette

SPECIAL EDITION™
Emotional, compelling stories that capture the intensity of living, loving and creating a family in today's world.

Silhouette®

Desire

A highly passionate, emotionally powerful and always provocative read.

Silhouette®
Where love comes alive™

Silhouette

INTIMATE MOMENTS™
A roller-coaster read that delivers romantic thrills in a world of suspense, adventure and more.

SILHOUETTE *Romance*

From first love to forever, these love stories are for today's woman with traditional values.

Visit Silhouette at www.eHarlequin.com

SILGENINT

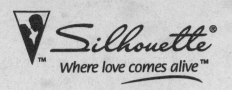

Where love comes alive™

From first love to forever, these love stories are
for today's woman with traditional values.

A highly passionate, emotionally powerful
and always provocative read.

V *Silhouette*°

SPECIAL EDITION™

Emotional, compelling stories that capture the
intensity of living, loving and creating a family in
today's world.

V *Silhouette*°

INTIMATE MOMENTS™

A roller-coaster read that delivers romantic thrills
in a world of suspense, adventure and more.

Visit Silhouette at www.eHarlequin.com

SDIR2